MW01141784

Naudsonce

AND OTHER SF

Naudsonce

AND OTHER SF

H. Beam Piper

ÆGYPAN PRESS

Naudsonce and Other SF
A publication of
Ægypan Press

www.aegypan.com

Table of Contents

Day of the Moron

*T*here were still, in 1968, a few people who were afraid of the nuclear power plant. Oldsters, in whom the term "atomic energy" produced semantic reactions associated with Hiroshima. Those who saw, in the towering steam-column above it, a tempting target for enemy — which still meant Soviet — bombers and guided missiles. Some of the Central Intelligence and F.B.I. people, who realized how futile even the most elaborate security measures were against a resourceful and suicidally determined saboteur. And a minority of engineers and nuclear physicists who remained unpersuaded that accidental blowups at nuclear-reaction plants were impossible.

Scott Melroy was among these last. He knew, as a matter of fact, that there had been several nasty, meticulously unpublicized, near-catastrophes at the Long Island Nuclear Reaction Plant, all involving the new Doernberg-Giardano breeder-reactors, and that there had been considerable carefully-hushed top-level acrimony before the Melroy Engineering Corporation had been given the contract to install the fully cybernetic control system intended to prevent a recurrence of such incidents.

That had been three months ago. Melroy and his people had moved in, been assigned sections of a couple of machine shops, set up an assembly shop and a set of plyboard-partitioned offices in a vacant warehouse just outside the reactor area, and tried to start work, only to run into the almost interminable procedural disputes and jurisdictional wranglings of the sort which he privately labeled "bureau bunk." It was only now that he was ready to begin work on the reactors.

He sat at his desk, in the inner of three successively smaller offices on the second floor of the converted warehouse, checking over a symbolic-logic analysis of a relay system and, at the same time, sharpening a pencil, his knife paring off tiny feathery shavings of wood. He was a tall, sparely-built, man of indeterminate age, with thinning sandy hair, a long Gaelic upper lip, and a wide, half-humorous, half-weary mouth; he wore an open-necked shirt, and an old and shabby leather jacket, to the left shoulder of which a few clinging flecks of paint showed where some military emblem had been, long ago. While his fingers worked with the jackknife and his eyes traveled over the page of closely-written symbols, his mind was reviewing the eight different ways in which one of the efficient but treacherous Doernberg-Giardano reactors could be allowed to reach critical mass, and he was wondering if there might not be some unsuspected ninth way. That was a possibility which always lurked in the back of his mind, and lately it had been giving him surrealistic nightmares.

"Mr. Melroy!" the box on the desk in front of him said suddenly, in a feminine voice. "Mr. Melroy, Dr. Rives is here."

Melroy picked up the handphone, thumbing on the switch.

"Dr. Rives?" he repeated.

"The psychologist who's subbing for Dr. von Heydenreich," the box told him patiently.

"Oh, yes. Show him in," Melroy said.

"Right away, Mr. Melroy," the box replied.

*R*eplacing the handphone, Melroy wondered, for a moment, why there had been a hint of suppressed amusement in his secretary's voice. Then the door opened and he stopped wondering. Dr. Rives wasn't a him; she was a her. Very attractive looking her, too — dark hair and eyes, rather long-oval features, clear, lightly tanned complexion, bright red lipstick put on with a micrometric exactitude that any engineer could appreciate. She was tall, within four inches of his own six-foot mark, and she wore a black tailored outfit, perfectly plain, which had probably cost around five hundred dollars and would have looked severe and mannish except that the figure under it curved and bulged in just the right places and to just the right degree.

Melroy rose, laying down knife and pencil and taking his pipe out of his mouth.

"Good afternoon," he greeted. "Dr. von Heydenreich gave me quite a favorable account of you — as far as it went. He might have included a few more data and made it more so. . . . Won't you sit down?"

The woman laid her handbag on the desk and took the visitor's chair, impish mirth sparking in her eyes.

"He probably omitted mentioning that the D. is for Doris," she suggested. "Suppose I'd been an Englishman with a name like Evelyn or Vivian?"

Melroy tried to visualize her as a male Englishman named Vivian, gave up, and grinned at her.

"Let this be a lesson," he said. "Inferences are to be drawn from objects, or descriptions of objects; never from verbal labels. Do you initial your first name just to see how people react when they meet you?"

"Well, no, though that's an amusing and sometimes instructive by-product. It started when I began contributing to some of the professional journals. There's still a little of what used to be called male sex-chauvinism among my colleagues, and some who would be favorably impressed with an article signed D. Warren Rives might snort in contempt at the same article signed Doris Rives."

"Well, fortunately, Dr. von Heydenreich isn't one of those," Melroy said. "How is the Herr Doktor, by the way, and just what happened to him? Miss Kourtakides merely told me that he'd been injured and was in a hospital in Pittsburgh."

"The Herr Doktor got shot," Doris Rives informed him. "With a charge of BB's, in a most indelicate portion of his anatomy. He was out hunting, the last day of small-game season, and somebody mistook him for a turkey. Nothing really serious, but he's face down in bed, cursing hideously in German, English, Russian, Italian and French, mainly because he's missing deer hunting."

"I might have known it," Melroy said in disgust. "The ubiquitous lame-brain with a dangerous mechanism. . . . I suppose he briefed you on what I want done, here?"

"Well, not too completely. I gathered that you want me to give intelligence tests, or aptitude tests, or something of the sort, to some of your employees. I'm not really one of these so-called industrial anthropologists," she explained. "Most of my work, for the past few years, has been for public-welfare organizations, with subnormal persons. I told him that, and he said that was why he selected me. He said one other thing. He said, 'I used to think Melroy had an obsession about fools; well, after stopping this load of shot, I'm beginning to think it's a good subject to be obsessed about.'"

Melroy nodded. "'Obsession' will probably do. 'Phobia' would be more exact. I'm afraid of fools, and the chance that I have one working for me, here, affects me like having a cobra crawling around my bedroom in the dark. I want you to locate any who might be in a gang of new men I've had to hire, so that I can get rid of them."

*A*nd just how do you define the term 'fool,' Mr. Melroy?" she asked. "Remember, it has no standard meaning. Republicans apply it to Democrats, and vice versa."

"Well, I apply it to people who do things without considering possible consequences. People who pepper distinguished Austrian psychologists in the pants-seat with turkey-shot, for a starter. Or people who push buttons to see what'll happen, or turn valves and twiddle with dial-knobs because they have nothing else to do with their hands. Or shoot insulators off power lines to see if they can hit them. People who don't know it's loaded. People who think warning signs are purely ornamental. People who play practical jokes. People who —"

"I know what you mean. Just day-before-yesterday, I saw a woman toss a cocktail into an electric heater. She didn't want to drink it, and she thought it would just go up in steam. The result was slightly spectacular."

"Next time, she won't do that. She'll probably throw her drink into a lead-ladle, if there's one around. Well, on a statistical basis, I'd judge that I have three or four such dud rounds among this new gang I've hired. I want you to put the finger on them, so I can bounce them before they blow the whole plant up, which could happen quite easily."

"That," Doris Rives said, "is not going to be as easy as it sounds. Ordinary intelligence-testing won't be enough. The woman I was speaking of has an I.Q. well inside the meaning of normal intelligence. She just doesn't use it."

"Sure." Melroy got a thick folder out of his desk and handed it across. "Heydenreich thought of that, too. He got this up for me, about five years ago. The intelligence test is based on the new French Sûreté test for mentally deficient criminals. Then there's a memory test, and tests for judgment and discrimination, semantic reactions, temperamental and emotional makeup, and general mental attitude."

She took the folder and leafed through it. "Yes, I see. I always liked this Sûreté test. And this memory test is a honey — 'One hen, two ducks, three squawking geese, four corpulent porpoises, five Limerick oysters, six pairs of Don Alfonso tweezers. . . .' I'd like to see some of these memory-course boys trying to make visual images of six pairs of Don Alfonso tweezers. And I'm going to make a copy of this word-association list. It's really a semantic reaction test; Korzybski would have loved it. And, of course, our old friend, the Rorschach Ink-Blots. I've always harbored the impious suspicion that you can prove almost anything you want to with that. But these question-suggestions for personal interview are really crafty. Did Heydenreich get them up himself?"

"Yes. And we have stacks and stacks of printed forms for the written portion of the test, and big cards to summarize each subject on. And we have a disk-recorder to use in the oral tests. There'll have to be a pretty complete record of each test, in case —"

*T*he office door opened and a bulky man with a black mustache entered, beating the snow from his overcoat with a battered porkpie hat and commenting blasphemously on the weather. He advanced into the room until he saw the woman in the chair beside the desk, and then started to back out.

"Come on in, Sid," Melroy told him. "Dr. Rives, this is our general foreman, Sid Keating. Sid, Dr. Rives, the new dimwit detector. Sid's in direct charge of personnel," he continued, "so you two'll be working together quite a bit."

"Glad to know you, doctor," Keating said. Then he turned to Melroy. "Scott, you're really going through with this, then?" he asked. "I'm afraid we'll have trouble, then."

"Look, Sid," Melroy said. "We've been all over that. Once we start work on the reactors, you and Ned Puryear and Joe Ricci and Steve Chalmers can't be everywhere at once. A cybernetic system will only do what it's been assembled to do, and if some quarter-wit assembles one of these things wrong —" He left the sentence dangling; both men knew what he meant.

Keating shook his head. "This union's going to bawl like a branded calf about it," he predicted. "And if any of the dear sirs and brothers get washed out —" That sentence didn't need to be completed, either.

"We have a right," Melroy said, "to discharge any worker who is, quote, of unsound mind, deficient mentality or emotional instability, unquote. It says so right in our union contract, in nice big print."

"Then they'll claim the tests are wrong."

"I can't see how they can do that," Doris Rives put in, faintly scandalized.

"Neither can I, and they probably won't either," Keating told her. "But they'll go ahead and do it. Why, Scott, they're pulling the Number One Doernberg-Giardano, tonight. By oh-eight-hundred, it ought to be cool enough to work on. Where will we hold the tests? Here?"

"We'll have to, unless we can get Dr. Rives security-cleared." Melroy turned to her. "Were you ever security-cleared by any Government agency?"

"Oh, yes. I was with Armed Forces Medical, Psychiatric Division, in Indonesia in '62 and '63, and I did some work with mental fatigue cases at Tonto Basin Research Establishment in '64."

Melroy looked at her sharply. Keating whistled.

"If she could get into Tonto Basin, she can get in here," he declared.

"I should think so. I'll call Colonel Bradshaw, the security officer."

"That way, we can test them right on the job," Keating was saying. "Take them in relays. I'll talk to Ben about it, and we'll work up some kind of a schedule." He turned to Doris Rives. "You'll need a wrist-Geiger, and a dosimeter. We'll furnish them," he told her. "I hope they don't try to make you carry a pistol, too."

"A pistol?" For a moment, she must have thought he was using some technical-jargon term, and then it dawned on her that he wasn't. "You mean — ?" She cocked her thumb and crooked her index finger.

"Yeah. A rod. Roscoe. The Equalizer. We all have to." He half-lifted one out of his side pocket. "We're all United States deputy marshals. They don't bother much with counterespionage, here, but they don't fool when it comes to countersabotage. Well, I'll get an order cut and posted. Be seeing you, doctor."

"Y ou think the union will make trouble about these tests?" she asked, after the general foreman had gone out.

"They're sure to," Melroy replied. "Here's the situation. I have about fifty of my own men, from Pittsburgh, here, but they can't work on the reactors because they don't belong to the Industrial Federation of Atomic Workers, and I can't just pay their initiation fees and union dues and get union cards for them, because admission to this union is on an annual quota basis, and this is December, and the quota's full. So I have to use them outside the reactor area, on fabrication and assembly work. And I have to hire through the union, and that's handled on a membership seniority basis, so I have to take what's thrown at me. That's why I was careful to get that clause I was quoting to Sid written into my contract.

"Now, here's what's going to happen. Most of the men'll take the test without protest, but a few of them'll raise the roof about it. Nothing burns a moron worse than to have somebody question his fractional intelligence. The odds are that the ones that yell the loudest about taking the test will be the ones who get scrubbed out, and when the test shows that they're deficient, they won't believe it. A moron simply cannot conceive of his being anything less than perfectly intelligent, anymore than a lunatic can conceive of his being less than perfectly sane. So they'll claim we're framing them, for an excuse to fire them. And the union will have to back them up, right or wrong, at least on the local level. That goes without saying. In any dispute, the employer is always wrong and the worker is always right, until proven otherwise. And that takes a lot of doing, believe me!"

"Well, if they're hired through the union, on a seniority basis, wouldn't they be likely to be experienced and competent workers?" she asked.

"Experienced, yes. That is, none of them has ever been caught doing anything downright calamitous . . . yet," Melroy replied. "The moron I'm afraid of can go on for years, doing routine work under supervision, and nothing'll happen. Then, some day, he does something on his own lame-brained initiative, and when he does, it's only at the whim of whatever gods there be that the result isn't a wholesale catastrophe. And people like that are the most serious threat facing our civilization today, atomic war not excepted."

Dr. Doris Rives lifted a delicately penciled eyebrow over that. Melroy, pausing to relight his pipe, grinned at her.

"You think that's the old obsession talking?" he asked. "Could be. But look at this plant, here. It generates every kilowatt of current used between Trenton and Albany, the New York metropolitan area included. Except for a few little storage-battery or Diesel generator systems, that couldn't handle one tenth of one percent of the barest minimum load, it's been the only source of electric current here since 1962, when the last coal-burning power plant was dismantled. Knock this plant out and you darken every house and office and factory and street in the area. You immobilize the elevators — think what that would mean in lower and midtown Manhattan alone. And the subways. And the new endless-belt conveyors that handle eighty percent of the city's freight traffic.

And the railroads — there aren't a dozen steam or Diesel locomotives left in the whole area. And the pump stations for water and gas and fuel oil. And seventy percent of the space-heating is electric, now. Why, you can't imagine what it'd be like. It's too gigantic. But what you can imagine would be a nightmare.

"You know, it wasn't so long ago, when every home lighted and heated itself, and every little industry was a self-contained unit, that a fool couldn't do great damage unless he inherited a throne or was placed in command of an army, and that didn't happen nearly as often as our leftist social historians would like us to think. But today, everything we depend upon is centralized, and vulnerable to blunder-damage. Even our food — remember that poisoned soft-drink horror in Chicago, in 1963; three thousand hospitalized and six hundred dead because of one man's stupid mistake at a bottling plant." He shook himself slightly, as though to throw off some shadow that had fallen over him, and looked at his watch. "Sixteen hundred. How did you get here? Fly your own plane?"

"No; I came by T.W.A. from Pittsburgh. I have a room at the new Midtown City hotel, on Forty-seventh Street: I had my luggage sent on there from the airport and came out on the Long Island subway."

"Fine. I have a room at Midtown City, myself, though I sleep here about half the time." He nodded toward a door on the left. "Suppose we go in and have dinner together. This cafeteria, here, is a horrible place. It's run by a dietitian instead of a chef, and everything's so white-enamel antiseptic that I swear I smell belladonna-icthyol ointment every time I go in the place. Wait here till I change clothes."

*A*t the Long Island plant, no one was concerned about espionage — neither the processes nor the equipment used there were secret — but the countersabotage security was fantastically thorough. Every person or scrap of material entering the reactor area was searched; the life-history of every man and woman employed there was known back to the cradle. A broad highway encircled it outside the fence, patrolled night and day by twenty General Stuart cavalry-tanks. There were a thousand soldiers, and three hundred Atomic Power Authority police, and only God knew how many F.B.I, and Central Intelligence undercover agents. Every supervisor and inspector and salaried technician was an armed United States deputy marshal. And nobody, outside the Department of Defense, knew how much radar and counter-rocket and fighter protection the place had, but the air-defense zone extended from Boston to Philadelphia and as far inland as Wilkes-Barre, Pennsylvania.

The Long Island Nuclear Power Plant, Melroy thought, had all the invulnerability of Achilles — and no more.

The six new Doernberg-Giardano breeder-reactors clustered in a circle inside a windowless concrete building at the center of the plant. Beside their primary purpose of plutonium production, they furnished heat for the seawater distillation and chemical extraction system, processing the water that was run through the steam boilers at the main power reactors, condensed, redistilled, and finally pumped, pure, into the water mains of New York. Safe outside the shielding, in a corner of a high-ceilinged room, was the plyboard-screened on-the-job office of the Melroy Engineering Corporation's timekeepers and foremen. Beyond, along the far wall, were the washroom and locker room and lunch room of the workmen.

Sixty or seventy men, mostly in white coveralls and all wearing identification badges and carrying dosimeters in their breast pockets and midget Geigers strapped to their wrists, were crowded about the bulletin-board in front of the makeshift office. There was a hum of voices — some perplexed or angry, but mostly good-humored and bantering. As Melroy and Doris Rives approached, the talking died out and the men turned. In the sudden silence, one voice, harshly strident, continued:

". . . do they think this is, anyhow? We don't hafta take none of that."

Somebody must have nudged the speaker, trying without success to hush him. The bellicose voice continued, and Melroy spotted the speaker — short, thickset, his arms jutting out at an angle from his body, his heavy features soured with anger.

"Like we was a lotta halfwits, 'r nuts, 'r some'n! Well, we don't hafta stand for this. They ain't got no right —"

Doris Rives clung tighter to Melroy's arm as he pushed a way for himself and her through the crowd and into the temporary office. Inside, they were met by a young man with a deputy marshal's badge on his flannel shirt and a .38 revolver on his hip.

"Ben Puryear: Dr. Rives," Melroy introduced. "Who's the mouthy character outside?"

"One of the roustabouts; name's Burris," Puryear replied. "Wash-room lawyer."

Melroy nodded. "You always get one or two like that. How're the rest taking it?"

Puryear shrugged. "About how you'd expect. A lot of kidding about who's got any intelligence to test. Burris seems to be the only one who's trying to make an issue out of it."

"Well, what are they doing ganged up here?" Melroy wanted to know. "It's past oh-eight-hundred; why aren't they at work?"

"Reactor's still too hot. Temperature and radioactivity both too high; radioactivity's still up around eight hundred REM's."

"Well, then, we'll give them all the written portion of the test together, and start the personal interviews and oral tests as soon as they're through." He turned to Doris Rives. "Can you give all of them the written test together?" he asked. "And can Ben help you — distributing forms, timing the test, seeing that there's no fudging, and collecting the forms when they're done?"

"Oh, yes; all they'll have to do is follow the printed instructions." She looked around. "I'll need a desk, and an extra chair for the interview subject."

"Right over here, doctor." Puryear said. "And here are the forms and cards, and the sound-recorder, and blank sound disks."

"Yes," Melroy added. "Be sure you get a recording of every interview and oral test; we may need them for evidence."

He broke off as a man in white coveralls came pushing into the office. He was a scrawny little fellow with a wide, loose-lipped mouth and a protuberant Adam's apple; beside his identity badge, he wore a two-inch celluloid button lettered: I.F.A.W. STEWARD.

"Wanta use the phone," he said. "Union business."

Melroy gestured toward a telephone on the desk beside him. The newcomer shook his head, twisting his mouth into a smirk.

"Not that one; the one with the whisper mouthpiece," he said. "This is private union business."

Melroy shrugged and indicated another phone. The man with the union steward's badge picked it up, dialed, and held a lengthy conversation into it, turning his head away in case Melroy might happen to be a lip reader. Finally he turned.

"Mr. Crandall wants to talk to you," he said, grinning triumphantly, the phone extended to Melroy.

The engineer picked up another phone, snapping a button on the base of it.

"Melroy here," he said.

Something on the line started going *bee-beep-beep* softly.

"Crandall, executive secretary, I.F.A.W.," the man on the other end of the line identified himself. "Is there a recorder going on this line?"

"Naturally," Melroy replied. "I record all business conversations; office routine."

"Mr. Melroy, I've been informed that you propose forcing our members in your employ to submit to some kind of a mental test. Is that correct?"

"Not exactly. I'm not able to force anybody to submit to anything against his will. If anybody objects to taking these tests, he can say so, and I'll have his time made out and pay him off."

"That's the same thing. A threat of dismissal is coercion, and if these men want to keep their jobs they'll have to take this test."

"Well, that's stated more or less correctly," Melroy conceded. "Let's just put it that taking — and passing — this test is a condition of employment. My contract with your union recognizes my right to establish standards of intelligence; that's implied by my recognized right to dismiss any person of 'unsound mind, deficient mentality or emotional instability.' Psychological testing is the only means of determining whether or not a person is classifiable in those terms."

"Then, in case the test purports to show that one of these men is, let's say, mentally deficient, you intend dismissing him?"

"With the customary two weeks' severance-pay, yes."

"Well, if you do dismiss anybody on those grounds, the union will have to insist on reviewing the grounds for dismissal."

"My contract with your union says nothing whatever about any right of review being reserved by the union in such cases. Only in cases of disciplinary dismissal, which this is not. I take the position that certain minimum standards of intelligence and mental stability are essentials in this sort of work, just as, say, certain minimum standards of literacy are essential in clerical work."

"Then you're going to make these men take these tests, whatever they are?"

"If they want to work for me, yes. And anybody who fails to pass them will be dropped from my payroll."

"And who's going to decide whether or not these men have successfully passed these tests?" Crandall asked. "You?"

"Good Lord, no! I'm an electronics engineer, not a psychologist. The tests are being given, and will be evaluated, by a graduate psychologist, Dr. D. Warren Rives, who has a diploma from the American Board of Psychiatry and Neurology and is a member of the American Psychological Association. Dr. Rives will be the final arbiter on who is or is not disqualified by these tests."

"Well, our man Koffler says you have some girl there to give the tests," Crandall accused.

"I suppose he means Dr. Rives," Melroy replied. "I can assure you, she is an extremely competent psychologist, however. She came to me most highly recommended by Dr. Karl von Heydenreich, who is not inclined to be careless with his recommendations."

"Well, Mr. Melroy, we don't want anymore trouble with you than we have to have," Crandall told him, "but we will insist on reviewing any dismissals which occur as a result of these tests."

"You can do that. I'd advise, first, that you read over the contract you signed with me. Get a qualified lawyer to tell you what we've agreed to and what we haven't. Was there anything else you wanted to talk about?. . . No?. . . Then good morning, Mr. Crandall."

He hung up. "All right; let's get on with it," he said. "Ben, you get them into the lunch room; there are enough tables and benches in there for everybody to take the written test in two relays."

"The union's gotta be represented while these tests is going on," the union steward announced. "Mr. Crandall says I'm to stay here an' watch what you do to these guys."

"This man working for us?" Melroy asked Puryear.

"Yes. Koffler, Julius. Electrical fitter; Joe Ricci's gang."

"All right. See to it that he gets placed in the first relay for the written test, and gets first turn for the orals. That way he can spend the rest of his time on duty here for the union, and will know in advance what the test is like." He turned to Koffler. "But understand this. You keep your mouth out of it. If you see anything that looks objectionable, make a note of it, but don't try to interfere."

The written tests, done on printed forms, required about twenty minutes. Melroy watched the process of oral testing and personal interviewing for a while, then picked up a big flashlight and dropped it into his overcoat pocket, preparatory to going out to inspect some equipment that had been assembled outside the reactor area and brought in. As he went out, Koffler was straddling a chair, glowering at Doris Rives and making occasional ostentatious notes on a pad.

*F*or about an hour, he poked around the newly assembled apparatus, checking the wiring, and peering into it. When he returned to the temporary office, the oral testing was still going on; Koffler was still on duty as watcher for the union, but the sport had evidently palled on him, for he was now studying a comic book.

Melroy left the reactor area and returned to the office in the converted area. During the midafternoon, somebody named Leighton called him from the Atomic Power Authority executive office, wanting to know what was the trouble between him and the I.F.A.W. and saying that a protest against his alleged high-handed and arbitrary conduct had been received from the union.

Melroy explained, at length. He finished: "You people have twenty Stuart tanks, and a couple of thousand soldiers and cops and under-cover-men, here, guarding against sabotage. Don't you realize that a workman who makes stupid or careless or impulsive mistakes is just as dangerous to the plant as any saboteur? If somebody shoots you through the head, it doesn't matter whether he planned to murder you for a year or just didn't know the gun was loaded; you're as dead one way as the other. I should think you'd thank me for trying to eliminate a serious source of danger."

"Now, don't misunderstand my position, Mr. Melroy," the other man hastened to say. "I sympathize with your attitude, entirely. But these people are going to make trouble."

"If they do, it'll be my trouble. I'm under contract to install this cybernetic system for you; you aren't responsible for my labor policy," Melroy replied. "Oh, have you had much to do with this man Crandall, yourself?"

"Have I had — !" Leighton sputtered for a moment. "I'm in charge of personnel, here; that makes me his top-priority target, all the time."

"Well, what sort of a character is he, anyhow? When I contracted with the I.F.A.W., my lawyer and their lawyer handled everything; I never even met him."

"Well — He has his job to do, the same as I have," Leighton said. "He does it conscientiously. But it's like this — anything a workman tells him is the truth, and anything an employer tells him is a dirty lie. Until proven differently, of course, but that takes a lot of doing. And he goes off half-cocked a lot of times. He doesn't stop to analyze situations very closely."

"That's what I was afraid of. Well, you tell him you don't have any control over my labor relations. Tell him to bring his gripes to me."

*A*t sixteen-thirty, Doris Rives came in, finding him still at his desk.

"I have the written tests all finished, and I have about twenty of the tests and interviews completed," she said. "I'll have to evaluate the results, though. I wonder if there's a vacant desk around here, anywhere, and a record player."

"Yes, sure. Ask Joan to fix you up; she'll find a place for you to work. And if you're going to be working late, I'll order some dinner for you from the cafeteria. I'm going to be here all evening, myself."

Sid Keating came in, a short while later, peeling out of his overcoat, jacket and shoulder holster.

"I don't think they got everything out of that reactor," he said. "Radioactivity's still almost active-normal — about eight hundred REM's — and the temperature's away up, too. That isn't lingering radiation; that's prompt radiation."

"Radioactivity hasn't dropped since morning; I'd think so, too," Melroy said. "What are they getting on the breakdown counter?"

"Mostly neutrons and alpha-particles. I talked to Fred Hausinger, the maintenance boss; he doesn't like it, either."

"Well, I'm no nuclear physicist," Melroy disclaimed, "but all that alpha stuff looks like a big chunk of Pu-239 left inside. What's Fred doing about it?"

"Oh, poking around inside the reactor with telemetered scanners and remote-control equipment. When I left, he had a gang pulling out graphite blocks with RC-tongs. We probably won't get a chance to work on it much before thirteen-hundred tomorrow." He unzipped a bulky brief case he had brought in under his arm and dumped papers onto his desk. "I still have this stuff to get straightened out, too."

"Had anything to eat? Then call the cafeteria and have them send up three dinners. Dr. Rives is eating here, too. Find out what she wants; I want pork chops."

"Uh-huh; Li'l Abner Melroy; po'k chops unless otherwise specified." Keating got up and went out into the middle office. As he opened the door. Melroy could hear a recording of somebody being given a word-association test.

*H*alf an hour later, when the food arrived, they spread their table on a relatively clear desk in the middle office. Doris Rives had finished evaluating the completed tests; after dinner, she intended going over the written portions of the uncompleted tests.

"How'd the finished tests come out?" Melroy asked her.

"Better than I'd expected. Only two washouts," she replied. "Harvey Burris and Julius Koffler."

"Oh, *no!*" Keating wailed. "The I.F.A.W. steward, and the loudest-mouthed I-know-my-rights boy on the job!"

"Well, wasn't that to be expected?" Melroy asked. "If you'd seen the act those two put on —"

"They're both inherently stupid, infantile, and deficient in reasoning ability and judgment," Doris said. "Koffler is a typical adolescent problem-child show-off type, and Burris is an almost perfect twelve-year-old schoolyard bully. They both have inferiority complexes long enough to step on. If the purpose of this test is what I'm led to believe it is, I can't, in professional good conscience, recommend anything but that you get rid of both of them."

"What Bob's getting at is that they're the very ones who can claim, with the best show of plausibility, that the test is just a pretext to fire them for union activities," Melroy explained. "And the worst of it is, they're the only ones."

"Maybe we can scrub out a couple more on the written tests alone. Then they'll have company," Keating suggested.

"No, I can't do that." Doris was firm on the point. "The written part of the test was solely for ability to reason logically. Just among the three of us, I know some university professors who'd flunk on that. But if the rest of the tests show stability, sense of responsibility, good judgment, and a tendency to think before acting, the subject can be classified as a safe and reliable workman."

"Well, then, let's don't say anything till we have the tests all finished," Keating proposed.

"No!" Melroy cried. "Every minute those two are on the job, there's a chance they may do something disastrous. I'll fire them at oh-eight-hundred tomorrow."

"All right," Keating shook his head. "I only work here. But don't say I didn't warn you."

*B*y 0930 the next morning, Keating's forebodings began to be realized. The first intimation came with a phone call to Melroy from Crandall, who accused him of having used the psychological tests as a fraudulent pretext for discharging Koffler and Burris for union activities. When Melroy rejected his demand that the two men be reinstated, Crandall demanded to see the records of the tests.

"They're here at my office," Melroy told him. "You're welcome to look at them, and hear recordings of the oral portions of the tests. But I'd advise you to bring a professional psychologist along, because unless you're a trained psychologist yourself, they're not likely to mean much to you."

"Oh, sure!" Crandall retorted. "They'd have to be unintelligible to ordinary people, or you couldn't get away with this frame-up! Well, don't worry, I'll be along to see them."

Within ten minutes, the phone rang again. This time it was Leighton, the Atomic Power Authority man.

"We're much disturbed about this dispute between your company and the I.F.A.W.," he began.

"Well, frankly, so am I," Melroy admitted. "I'm here to do a job, not play Hatfields and McCoys with this union. I've had union trouble before, and it isn't fun. You're the gentleman who called me last evening, aren't you? Then you understand my position in the matter."

"Certainly, Mr. Melroy. I was talking to Colonel Bradshaw, the security officer, last evening. He agrees that a stupid or careless workman is, under some circumstances, a more serious threat to security than any saboteur. And we realize fully how dangerous those Doernberg-Giardanos are, and how much more dangerous they'd be if these cybernetic controls were improperly assembled. But this man Crandall is talking about calling a strike."

"Well, let him. In the first place, it'd be against me, not against the Atomic Power Authority. And, in the second place, if he does and it goes to Federal mediation, his demand for the reinstatement of those men will be thrown out, and his own organization will have to disavow his action, because he'll be calling the strike against his own contract."

"Well, I hope so." Leighton's tone indicated that the hope was rather dim. "I wish you luck; you're going to need it."

*W*ithin the hour, Crandall arrived at Melroy's office. He was a young man; he gave Melroy the impression of having recently seen military service; probably in the Indonesian campaign of '62 and '63; he also seemed a little cocky and oversure of himself.

"Mr. Melroy, we're not going to stand for this," he began, as soon as he came into the room. "You're using these so-called tests as a pretext for getting rid of Mr. Koffler and Mr. Burris because of their legitimate union activities."

"Who gave you that idea?" Melroy wanted to know. "Koffler and Burris?"

"That's the complaint they made to me, and it's borne out by the facts," Crandall replied. "We have on record at least half a dozen complaints that Mr. Koffler has made to us about different unfair work-assignments, improper working conditions, inequities in allotting overtime work, and other infractions of union-shop conditions, on behalf of Mr. Burris. So you decided to get rid of both of them, and you think you can use this clause in our contract with your company about persons of deficient intelligence. The fact is, you're known to have threatened on several occasions to get rid of both of them."

"I am?" Melroy looked at Crandall curiously, wondering if the latter were serious, and deciding that he was. "You must believe *anything* those people tell you. Well, they lied to you if they told you that."

"Naturally that's what you'd say," Crandall replied. "But how do you account for the fact that those two men, and only those two men, were dismissed for alleged deficient intelligence?"

"The tests aren't all made," Melroy replied. "Until they are, you can't say that they are the only ones disqualified. And if you look over the records of the tests, you'll see where Koffler and Burris failed and the others passed. Here." He laid the pile of written-test forms and the summary and evaluation sheets on the desk. "Here's Koffler's, and here's Burris'; these are the ones of the men who passed the test. Look them over if you want to."

Crandall examined the forms and summaries for the two men who had been discharged, and compared them with several random samples from the satisfactory pile.

"Why, this stuff's a lot of gibberish!" he exclaimed indignantly. "This thing, here: . . . five Limerick oysters, six pairs of Don Alfonso tweezers, seven hundred Macedonian warriors in full battle array, eight golden crowns from the ancient, secret crypts of Egypt, nine lymphatic, sympathetic, peripatetic old men on crutches, and ten revolving heliotropes from the Ipsy-Wipsy Institute!' Great Lord, do you actually mean that you're using this stuff as an excuse for depriving men of their jobs?"

"I warned you that you should have brought a professional psychologist along," Melroy reminded him. "And maybe you ought to get Koffler and Burris to repeat their complaints on a lie-detector, while you're at it. They took the same tests, in the same manner, as any of the others. They just didn't have the mental equipment to cope with them and the others did. And for that reason, I won't run the risk of having them working on this job."

"That's just your word against theirs," Crandall insisted obstinately. "Their complaint is that you framed this whole thing up to get rid of them."

"Why, I didn't even know who either of them were, until yesterday morning."

"That's not the way they tell it," Crandall retorted. "They say you and Keating have been out to get them ever since they were hired. You and your supervisors have been persecuting both of those men systematically. The fact that Burris has had grounds for all these previous complaints proves that."

"It proves that Burris has a persecution complex, and that Koffler's credulous enough to believe him," Melroy replied. "And that tends to confirm the results of the tests they failed to pass."

"Oh, so that's the line you're taking. You persecute a man, and then say he has a persecution complex if he recognizes the fact. Well, you're not going to get away with it, that's all I have to say to you." Crandall flung the test-sheet he had been holding on to the desk. "That stuff's not worth the paper it's scribbled on!" He turned on his heel in an automatically correct about-face and strode out of the office.

*M*elroy straightened out the papers and put them away, then sat down at his desk, filling and lighting his pipe. He was still working at 1215 when Ben Puryear called him.

"They walked out on us," he reported. "Harry Crandall was out here talking to them, and at noon the whole gang handed in their wrist-Geigers and dosimeters and cleared out their lockers. They say they aren't coming back till Burris and Koffler come back to work with them."

"Then they aren't coming back, period," Melroy replied. "Crandall was to see me, a couple of hours ago. He tells me that Burris and Koffler told him that we've been persecuting Burris; discriminating against him. You know of anything that really happened that might make them think anything like that?"

"No. Burris is always yelling about not getting enough overtime work, but you know how it is: he's just a roustabout, a common laborer. Any overtime work that has to be done is usually skilled labor on this job. We generally have a few roustabouts to help out, but he's been allowed to make overtime as much as any of the others."

"Will the time-records show that?"

"They ought to. I don't know what he and Koffler told Crandall, but whatever it was, I'll bet they were lying."

"That's all right, then. How's the reactor, now?"

"Hausinger says the count's down to safe limits, and the temperature's down to inactive normal. He and his gang found a big chunk of plutonium, about one-quarter CM, inside. He got it out."

"All right. Tell Dr. Rives to gather up all her completed or partially completed test records and come out to the office. You and the others stay on the job; we may have some men for you by this afternoon; tomorrow morning certainly."

He hung up, then picked up the communicator phone and called his secretary.

"Joan, is Sid Keating out there? Send him in, will you?"

Keating, when he entered, was wearing the lugubriously gratified expression appropriate to the successful prophet of disaster.

"All right, Cassandra," Melroy greeted him. "I'm not going to say you didn't warn me. Look. This strike is illegal. It's a violation of the Federal Labor Act of 1958, being called without due notice of intention, without preliminary negotiation, and without two weeks' time-allowance."

"They're going to claim that it isn't a strike. They're going to call it a 'spontaneous work-stoppage.'"

"Aah! I hope I can get Crandall on record to that effect; I'll fire every one of those men for leaving their work without permission and absence from duty without leave. How many of our own men, from Pittsburgh, do we have working in these machine shops and in the assembly shop here? About sixty?"

"Sixty-three. Why? You're not going to use them to work on the reactor, are you?"

"I just am. They're all qualified cybernetics technicians; they can do this work better than this gang we've had to hire here. Just to be on the safe side, I'm promoting all of them, as of oh-eight-hundred this morning, to assistant gang-foremen, on salaries. That'll take them outside union jurisdiction."

"But how about our contract with the I.F.A.W.?"

"That's been voided, by Crandall's own act, in interfering with the execution of our contract with the Atomic Power Authority. You know what I think? I think the I.F.A.W. front office is going to have to disavow this. It'll hurt them to do it, but they'll have to. Crandall's put them in the middle on this."

"How about security clearance for our own men?"

"Nothing to that," Melroy said. "Most of them are security-cleared, already, from the work we did installing that counter-rocket control system on the U.S.S. *Alaska,* and the work we did on that symbolic-logic computer for the Philadelphia Project. It may take all day to get the red tape unwound, but I think we can be ready to start by oh-eight-hundred tomorrow."

By the time Keating had rounded up all the regular Melroy Engineering Corporation employees and Melroy had talked to Colonel Bradshaw about security-clearance, it was 1430. A little later, he was called on the phone by Leighton, the Atomic Power Authority man.

"Melroy, what are you trying to do?" the Power Authority man demanded. "Get this whole plant struck shut? The I.F.A.W.'s mad-der than a shot-stung bobcat. They claim you're going to bring in strike-breakers; they're talking about picketing the whole reactor area."

"News gets around fast, here, doesn't it?" Melroy commented. He told Leighton what he had in mind. The Power Authority man was considerably shaken before he had finished.

"But they'll call a strike on the whole plant! Have you any idea what that would mean?"

"Certainly I have. They'll either call it in legal form, in which case the whole thing will go to mediation and get aired, which is what I want, or they'll pull a Pearl Harbor on you, the way they did on me. And in that case, the President will have to intervene, and they'll fly in technicians from some of the Armed Forces plants to keep this place running. And in that case, things'll get settled that much quicker. This Crandall thinks these men I fired are martyrs, and he's preaching a crusade. He ought to carry an *advocatus diaboli* on his payroll, to scrutinize the qualifications of his martyrs, before he starts canonizing them."

A little later, Doris Rives came into the office, her hands full of papers and cards.

"I have twelve more tests completed," she reported. "Only one washout."

Melroy laughed. "Doctor, they're all washed out," he told her. "It seems there was an additional test, and they all flunked it.

Evinced willingness to follow unwise leadership and allow themselves to be talked into improper courses of action. You go on in
to New York, and take all the test-material, including sound records, with you. Stay at the hotel — your pay will go on — till I
need you. There'll be a Federal Mediation hearing in a day or so."

He had two more telephone calls. The first, at 1530, was from
Leighton. Melroy suspected that the latter had been medicating
his morale with a couple of stiff drinks: his voice was almost jaunty.

"Well, the war's on," he announced. "The I.F.A.W.'s walking out
on the whole plant, at oh-eight-hundred tomorrow."

"In violation of the Federal Labor Act, Section Eight, para-
graphs four and five," Melroy supplemented. "Crandall really has
stuck his neck in the guillotine. What's Washington doing?"

"President Hartley is ordering Navy personnel flown in from
Kennebunkport Reaction Lab; they will be here by about oh-three-
hundred tomorrow. And a couple of Federal mediators are coming
in to La Guardia at seventeen hundred; they're going to hold
preliminary hearings at the new Federal Building on Washington
Square beginning twenty hundred. A couple of I.F.A.W. negotiators
are coming in from the national union headquarters at Oak Ridge:
they should be getting in about the same time. You'd better be on
hand, and have Dr. Rives there with you. There's a good chance
this thing may get cleared up in a day or so."

"I will undoubtedly be there, complete with Dr. Rives," Melroy
replied. "It will be a pleasure!"

*A*n hour later, Ben Puryear called from the reactor area, his
voice strained with anger.

"Scott, do you know what those —" He gargled obscenities for
a moment. "You know what they've done? They've re-packed the
Number One Doernberg-Giardano; got a chain-reaction started
again."

"Who?"

"Fred Hausinger's gang. Apparently at Harry Crandall's orders.
The excuse was that it would be unsafe to leave the reactor in its
dismantled condition during a prolonged shutdown — they were
assuming, I suppose, that the strike would be allowed to proceed
unopposed — but of course the real reason was that they wanted
to get a chain-reaction started to keep our people from working
on the reactor."

"Well, didn't Hausinger try to stop them?"

"Not very hard. I asked him what he had that deputy marshal's badge on his shirt and that Luger on his hip for, but he said he had orders not to use force, for fear of prejudicing the mediators."

Melroy swore disgustedly. "All right. Gather up all our private papers, and get Steve and Joe, and come on out. We only work here — when we're able."

*D*oris Rives was waiting on the street level when Melroy reached the new Federal Building, in what had formerly been the Greenwich Village district of Manhattan, that evening. She had a heavy brief case with her, which he took.

"I was afraid I'd keep you waiting," she said. "I came down from the hotel by cab, and there was a frightful jam at Fortieth Street, and another one just below Madison Square."

"Yes, it gets worse every year. Pardon my obsession, but nine times out of ten — ninety-nine out of a hundred — it's the fault of some fool doing something stupid. Speaking about doing stupid things, though — I did one. Forgot to take that gun out of my overcoat pocket, and didn't notice that I had it till I was on the subway, coming in. Have a big flashlight in the other pocket, but that doesn't matter. What I'm worried about is that somebody'll find out I have a gun and raise a howl about my coming armed to a mediation hearing."

The hearing was to be held in one of the big conference rooms on the forty-second floor. Melroy was careful to remove his overcoat and lay it on a table in the corner, and then help Doris off with hers and lay it on top of his own. There were three men in the room when they arrived: Kenneth Leighton, the Atomic Power Authority man, fiftyish, acquiring a waistline bulge and losing his hair: a Mr. Lyons, tall and slender, with white hair; and a Mr. Quillen, considerably younger, with plastic-rimmed glasses. The latter two were the Federal mediators. All three had been lounging in armchairs, talking about the new plays on Broadway. They all rose when Melroy and Doris Rives came over to join them.

"We mustn't discuss business until the others get here," Leighton warned. "It's bad enough that all three of us got here ahead of them; they'll be sure to think we're trying to take an unfair advantage of them. I suppose neither of you have had time to see any of the new plays."

Fortunately, Doris and Melroy had gone to the theater after dinner, the evening-before-last; they were able to join the conversation. Young Mr. Quillen wanted Doris Rives' opinion, as a psychologist, of the mental processes of the heroine of the play they had seen; as nearly as she could determine, Doris replied, the heroine in question had exhibited nothing even loosely describable as mental processes of any sort. They were still on the subject when the two labor negotiators, Mr. Cronnin and Mr. Fields, arrived. Cronnin was in his sixties, with the nearsighted squint and compressed look of concentration of an old-time precision machinist; Fields was much younger, and sported a Phi Beta Kappa key.

Lyons, who seemed to be the senior mediator, thereupon called the meeting to order and they took their places at the table.

"Now, gentlemen — and Dr. Rives — this will be simply an informal discussion, so that everybody can see what everybody else's position in the matter is. We won't bother to make a sound recording. Then, if we have managed to reach some common understanding of the question this evening, we can start the regular hearing say at thirteen hundred tomorrow. Is that agreeable?"

It was. The younger mediator, Quillen, cleared his throat.

"It seems, from our information, that this entire dispute arises from the discharge, by Mr. Melroy, of two of his employees, named Koffler and Burris. Is that correct?"

"Well, there's also the question of the Melroy Engineering Corporation's attempting to use strike-breakers, and the Long Island Atomic Power Authority's having condoned this unfair employment practice," Cronnin said, acidly.

"And there's also the question of the I.F.A.W.'s calling a Pearl Harbor strike on my company," Melroy added.

"We resent that characterization!" Cronnin retorted.

"It's a term in common usage; it denotes a strike called without warning or declaration of intention, which this was," Melroy told him.

"And there's also the question of the I.F.A.W. calling a general strike, in illegal manner, at the Long Island Reaction Plant," Leighton spoke up. "On sixteen hours' notice."

"Well, that wasn't the fault of the I.F.A.W. as an organization," Fields argued. "Mr. Cronnin and I are agreed that the walk-out date should be postponed for two weeks, in accordance with the provisions of the Federal Labor Act."

"Well, how about my company?" Melroy wanted to know. "Your I.F.A.W. members walked out on me, without any notice whatever, at twelve hundred today. Am I to consider that an act of your union, or will you disavow it so that I can fire all of them for quitting without permission?"

"And how about the action of members of your union, acting on instructions from Harry Crandall, in re-packing the Number One Doernberg-Giardano breeder-reactor at our plant, after the plutonium and the U-238 and the neutron-source containers had been removed, in order to re-initiate a chain reaction to prevent Mr. Melroy's employees from working on the reactor?" Leighton demanded. "Am I to understand that the union sustains that action, too?"

"I hadn't known about that," Fields said, somewhat startled.

"Neither had I," Cronnin added. "When did it happen?"

"About sixteen hundred today," Melroy told him.

"We were on the plane from Oak Ridge, then," Fields declared. "We know nothing about that."

"Well, are you going to take the responsibility for it, or aren't you?" Leighton insisted.

Lyons, who had been toying with a small metal paperweight, rapped on the table with it.

"Gentlemen," he interrupted. "We're trying to cover too many subjects at once. I suggest that we confine ourselves, at the beginning, to the question of the dismissal of these men, Burris and Koffler. If we find that the I.F.A.W. has a legitimate grievance in what we may call the Burris-Koffler question, we can settle that and then go on to these other questions."

"I'm agreeable to that," Melroy said.

"So are we," Cronnin nodded.

"All right, then. Since the I.F.A.W. is the complaining party in this question, perhaps you gentlemen should state the grounds for your complaints."

Fields and Cronnin exchanged glances: Cronnin nodded to Fields and the latter rose. The two employees in question, he stated, had been the victims of discrimination and persecution because of union activities. Koffler was the union shop-steward for the men employed by the Melroy Engineering Corporation, and Burris had been active in bringing complaints about unfair employment practices. Furthermore, it was the opinion of the I.F.A.W. that the psychological tests imposed on their members had been a fraudulent pretext for dismissing these two men, and, in any case, the practice of compelling workers to submit to such tests was insulting, degrading, and not a customary condition of employment.

With that, he sat down. Melroy was on his feet at once.

"I'll deny those statements, categorically and seriatim," he replied. "They are based entirely upon misrepresentations made by the two men who were disqualified by the tests and dropped from my payroll because of being, in the words of my contract with your union, 'persons of unsound mind, deficient intelligence and/or emotional instability.' What happened is that your local official, Crandall, accepted everything they told him uncritically, and you accepted everything Crandall told you, in the same spirit.

"Before I go on," Melroy continued, turning to Lyons, "have I your permission to let Dr. Rives explain about these tests, herself, and tell how they were given and evaluated?"

*P*ermission granted by Lyons, Doris Rives rose. At some length, she explained the nature and purpose of the tests, and her method of scoring and correlating them.

"Well, did Mr. Melroy suggest to you that any specific employee or employees of his were undesirable and ought to be eliminated?" Fields asked.

"Certainly not!" Doris Rives became angry. "And if he had, I'd have taken the first plane out of here. That suggestion is insulting! And for your information, I never met Mr. Melroy before day-before-yesterday afternoon; I am not dependent upon him for anything; I took this job as an accommodation to Dr. Karl von Heydenreich, who ordinarily does such work for the Melroy company, and I'm losing money by remaining here. Does that satisfy you?"

"Yes, it does," Fields admitted. He was obviously impressed by mention of the distinguished Austrian psychologist's name. "If I may ask Mr. Melroy a question: I gather that these tests are given to all your employees. Why do you demand such an extraordinary level of intelligence from your employees, even common laborers?"

"Extraordinary?" Melroy echoed. "If the standards established by those tests are extraordinary, then God help this country; we are becoming a race of morons! I'll leave that statement to Dr. Rives for confirmation; she's already pointed out that all that is required to pass those tests is ordinary adult mental capacity.

"My company specializes in cybernetic-control systems," he continued. "In spite of a lot of misleading colloquial jargon about 'thinking machines' and 'giant brains,' a cybernetic system doesn't really think. It only does what it's been designed *and built* to do, and if somebody builds a mistake into it, it will automatically and infallibly repeat that mistake in practice."

"He's right," Cronnin said. "The men that build a machine like that have got to be as smart as the machine's supposed to be, or the machine'll be as dumb as they are."

Fields turned on him angrily. "Which side are you supposed to be on, anyhow?" he demanded.

"You're probably a lawyer," Melroy said. "But I'll bet Mr. Cronnin's an old reaction-plant man." Cronnin nodded unthinkingly in confirmation. "All right, then. Ask him what those Doernberg-Giardanos are like. And then let me ask you: Suppose some moron fixed up something that would go wrong, or made the wrong kind of a mistake himself, around one of those reactors?"

It was purely a rhetorical question, but, much later, when he would have time to think about it, Scott Melroy was to wonder if ever in history such a question had been answered so promptly and with such dramatic calamitousness.

Three seconds after he stopped speaking, the lights went out.

*F*or a moment, they were silent and motionless. Then somebody across the table from Melroy began to say, "What the devil — ?" Doris Rives, beside him, clutched his arm. At the head of the table, Lyons was fuming impatiently, and Kenneth Leighton snapped a pocket-lighter and held it up.

The Venetian-screened windows across the room faced east. In the flicker of the lighter, Melroy made his way around to them and drew open the slats of one, looking out. Except for the headlights of cars, far down in the street, and the lights of ships in the harbor, the city was completely blacked out. But there was one other, horrible, light far away at the distant tip of Long Island — a huge ball of flame, floating upward at the tip of a column of fiery gas. As he watched, there were twinkles of unbearable brightness at the base of the pillar of fire, spreading into awesome sheet-flashes, and other fireballs soared up. Then the sound and the shock-wave of the first blast reached them.

"The main power-reactors, too," Melroy said to himself, not realizing that he spoke audibly. "Too well shielded for the blast to get them, but the heat melted the fissionables down to critical mass."

Leighton, the lighter still burning, was beside him, now.

"That's not — God, it can't be anything else! Why, the whole plant's gone! There aren't enough other generators in this area to handle a hundredth of the demand."

"And don't blame that on my alleged strike-breakers," Melroy warned. "They hadn't got security-cleared to enter the reactor area when this happened."

"What do you think happened?" Cronnin asked. "One of the Doernberg-Giardanos let go?"

"Yes. Your man Crandall. If he survived that, it's his bad luck," Melroy said grimly. "Last night, while Fred Hausinger was pulling the fissionables and radioactives out of the Number One breeder, he found a big nugget of Pu-239, about one-quarter CM. I don't know what was done with it, but I do know that Crandall had the maintenance gang repack that reactor, to keep my people from working on it. Nobody'll ever find out just what happened, but they were in a hurry; they probably shoved things in any old way. Somehow, that big subcritical nugget must have got back in, and the breeding-cans, which were pretty ripe by that time, must have been shoved in too close to it and to one another. You know how fast those D-G's work. It just took this long to build up CM for a bomb-type reaction. You remember what I was saying before the lights went out? Well, it happened. Some moron — some untested and undetected moron — made the wrong kind of a mistake."

"Too bad about Crandall. He was a good kid, only he didn't stop to think often enough," Cronnin said. "Well, I guess the strike's off, now; that's one thing."

"But all those people, out there!" Womanlike, Doris Rives was thinking particularly rather than generally and of humans rather than abstractions. "It must have killed everybody for miles around."

Sid Keating, Melroy thought. And Joe Ricci, and Ben Puryear, and Steve Chalmers, and all the workmen whom he had brought here from Pittsburgh, to their death. Then he stopped thinking about them. It didn't do any good to think of men who'd been killed; he'd learned that years ago, as a kid second lieutenant in Korea. The people to think about were the millions in Greater New York, and up the Hudson Valley to Albany, and as far south as Trenton, caught without light in the darkness, without heat in the dead of winter, without power in subways and skyscrapers and on railroads and interurban lines.

He turned to the woman beside him.

"Doris, before you could get your Board of Psychiatry and Neurology diploma, you had to qualify as a regular M.D., didn't you?" he asked.

"Why, yes —"

"Then you'd better report to the nearest hospital. Any doctor at all is going to be desperately needed, for the next day or so. Me, I still have a reserve major's commission in the Army Corps of Engineers. They're probably calling up reserve officers, with any radios that are still working. Until I hear differently, I'm ordering myself on active duty as of now." He looked around. "Anybody know where the nearest Army headquarters is?"

"There's a recruiting station down on the thirty-something floor," Quillen said. "It's probably closed, now, though."

"Ground Defense Command; Midtown City," Leighton said. "They have a medical section of their own; they'll be glad to get Dr. Rives, too."

Melroy helped her on with her coat and handed her her handbag, then shrugged into his own overcoat and belted it about him, the weight of the flashlight and the automatic sagging the pockets. He'd need both, the gun as much as the light — New York had more than its share of vicious criminals, to whom this power-failure would be a perfect devilsend. Handing Doris the light, he let her take his left arm. Together, they left the room and went down the hallway to the stairs and the long walk to the darkened street below, into a city that had suddenly been cut off from its very life-energy. A city that had put all its eggs in one basket, and left the basket in the path of any blundering foot.

Police Operation

". . . there may be something in the nature of an occult police force, which operates to divert human suspicions, and to supply explanations that are good enough for whatever, somewhat in the nature of minds, human beings have — or that, if there be occult mischief makers and occult ravagers, they may be of a world also of other beings that are acting to check them, and to explain them, not benevolently, but to divert suspicion from themselves, because they, too, may be exploiting life upon this earth, but in ways more subtle, and in orderly, or organized, fashion."

Charles Fort: "LO!"

*J*ohn Strawmyer stood, an irate figure in faded overalls and sweat-whitened black shirt, apart from the others, his back to the weathered farm-buildings and the line of yellowing woods and the cirrus-streaked blue October sky. He thrust out a work-gnarled hand accusingly.

"That there heifer was worth two hund'rd, two hund'rd an' fifty dollars!" he clamored. "An' that there dog was just like one uh the fam'ly; An' now look at'm! I don't like t' use profane language, but you'ns gotta *do* some'n about this!"

Steve Parker, the district game protector, aimed his Leica at the carcass of the dog and snapped the shutter. "We're doing something about it," he said shortly. Then he stepped ten feet to the left and edged around the mangled heifer, choosing an angle for his camera shot.

The two men in the grey whipcords of the State police, seeing that Parker was through with the dog, moved in and squatted to examine it. The one with the triple chevrons on his sleeves took it by both forefeet and flipped it over on its back. It had been a big brute, of nondescript breed, with a rough black-and-brown coat. Something had clawed it deeply about the head, its throat was slashed transversely several times, and it had been disemboweled by a single slash that had opened its belly from breastbone to tail. They looked at it carefully, and then went to stand beside Parker while he photographed the dead heifer. Like the dog, it had been talon-raked on either side of the head, and its throat had been slashed deeply several times. In addition, flesh had been torn from one flank in great strips.

"I can't kill a bear outa season, no!" Strawmyer continued his plaint. "But a bear comes an' kills my stock an' my dog; that there's all right! That's the kinda deal a farmer always gits, in this state! I don't like t' use profane language —"

"Then don't!" Parker barked at him, impatiently. "Don't use any kind of language. Just put in your claim and shut up!" He turned to the men in whipcords and grey Stetsons. "You boys seen everything?" he asked. "Then let's go."

*T*hey walked briskly back to the barnyard, Strawmyer following them, still vociferating about the wrongs of the farmer at the hands of a cynical and corrupt State government. They climbed into the State police car, the sergeant and the private in front and Parker into the rear, laying his camera on the seat beside a Winchester carbine.

"Weren't you pretty short with that fellow, back there, Steve?" the sergeant asked as the private started the car.

"Not too short. 'I don't like t' use profane language,'" Parker mimicked the bereaved heifer owner, and then he went on to specify: "I'm morally certain that he's shot at least four illegal deer in the last year. When and if I ever get anything on him, he's going to be sorrier for himself then he is now."

"They're the characters that always beef their heads off," the sergeant agreed. "You think that whatever did this was the same as the others?"

"Yes. The dog must have jumped it while it was eating at the heifer. Same superficial scratches about the head, and deep cuts on the throat or belly. The bigger the animal, the farther front the big slashes occur. Evidently something grabs them by the head with front claws, and slashes with hind claws; that's why I think it's a bobcat."

"You know," the private said, "I saw a lot of wounds like that during the war. My outfit landed on Mindanao, where the guerrillas had been active. And this looks like bolo-work to me."

"The surplus-stores are full of machetes and jungle knives," the sergeant considered. "I think I'll call up Doc Winters, at the County Hospital, and see if all his squirrel-fodder is present and accounted for."

"But most of the livestock was eaten at, like the heifer," Parker objected.

"By definition, nuts have abnormal tastes," the sergeant replied. "Or the eating might have been done later, by foxes."

"I hope so; that'd let me out," Parker said.

"Ha, listen to the man!" the private howled, stopping the car at the end of the lane. "He thinks a nut with a machete and a Tarzan complex is just good clean fun. Which way, now?"

"Well, let's see." The sergeant had unfolded a quadrangle sheet; the game protector leaned forward to look at it over his shoulder. The sergeant ran a finger from one to another of a series of variously colored crosses which had been marked on the map.

"Monday night, over here on Copperhead Mountain, that cow was killed," he said. "The next night, about ten o'clock, that sheepflock was hit, on this side of Copperhead, right about here. Early Wednesday night, that mule got slashed up in the woods back of the Weston farm. It was only slightly injured; must have kicked the whatzit and got away, but the whatzit wasn't too badly hurt, because a few hours later, it hit that turkey-flock on the Rhymer farm. And last night, it did that." He jerked a thumb over his shoulder at the Strawmyer farm. "See, following the ridges, working toward the southeast, avoiding open ground, killing only at night. Could be a bobcat, at that."

"Or Jink's maniac with the machete," Parker agreed. "Let's go up by Hindman's gap and see if we can see anything."

*T*hey turned, after a while, into a rutted dirt road, which deteriorated steadily into a grass-grown track through the woods. Finally, they stopped, and the private backed off the road. The three men got out; Parker with his Winchester, the sergeant checking the drum of a Thompson, and the private pumping a buckshot shell into the chamber of a riot gun. For half an hour, they followed the brush-grown trail beside the little stream; once, they passed a dark grey commercial-model jeep, backed to one side. Then they came to the head of the gap.

A man, wearing a tweed coat, tan field boots, and khaki breeches, was sitting on a log, smoking a pipe; he had a bolt-action rifle across his knees, and a pair of binoculars hung from his neck. He seemed about thirty years old, and any bobby-soxer's idol of the screen would have envied him the handsome regularity of his strangely immobile features. As Parker and the two State policemen approached, he rose, slinging his rifle, and greeted them.

"Sergeant Haines, isn't it?" he asked pleasantly. "Are you gentlemen out hunting the critter, too?"

"Good afternoon, Mr. Lee. I thought that was your jeep I saw, down the road a little." The sergeant turned to the others. "Mr. Richard Lee; staying at the old Kinchwalter place, the other side of Rutter's Fort. This is Mr. Parker, the district game protector. And Private Zinkowski." He glanced at the rifle. "Are you out hunting for it, too?"

"Yes, I thought I might find something, up here. What do you think it is?"

"I don't know," the sergeant admitted. "It could be a bobcat. Canada lynx. Jink, here, has a theory that it's some escapee from the paper-doll factory, with a machete. Me, I hope not, but I'm not ignoring the possibility."

The man with the matinee-idol's face nodded. "It could be a lynx. I understand they're not unknown, in this section."

"We paid bounties on two in this county, in the last year," Parker said. "Odd rifle you have, there; mind if I look at it?"

"Not at all." The man who had been introduced as Richard Lee unslung and handed it over. "The chamber's loaded," he cautioned.

"I never saw one like this," Parker said. "Foreign?"

"I think so. I don't know anything about it; it belongs to a friend of mine, who loaned it to me. I think the action's German, or Czech; the rest of it's a custom job, by some West Coast gunmaker. It's chambered for some ultra-velocity wildcat load."

The rifle passed from hand to hand; the three men examined it in turn, commenting admiringly.

"You find anything, Mr. Lee?" the sergeant asked, handing it back.

"Not a trace." The man called Lee slung the rifle and began to dump the ashes from his pipe. "I was along the top of this ridge for about a mile on either side of the gap, and down the other side as far as Hindman's Run; I didn't find any tracks, or any indication of where it had made a kill."

The game protector nodded, turning to Sergeant Haines.

"There's no use us going any farther," he said. "Ten to one, it followed that line of woods back of Strawmyer's, and crossed over to the other ridge. I think our best bet would be the hollow at the head of Lowrie's Run. What do you think?"

The sergeant agreed. The man called Richard Lee began to refill his pipe methodically.

"I think I shall stay here for a while, but I believe you're right. Lowrie's Run, or across Lowrie's Gap into Coon Valley," he said.

*A*fter Parker and the State policemen had gone, the man whom they had addressed as Richard Lee returned to his log and sat smoking, his rifle across his knees. From time to time, he glanced at his wrist watch and raised his head to listen. At length, faint in the distance, he heard the sound of a motor starting.

Instantly, he was on his feet. From the end of the hollow log on which he had been sitting, he produced a canvas musette-bag. Walking briskly to a patch of damp ground beside the little stream, he leaned the rifle against a tree and opened the bag. First, he took out a pair of gloves of some greenish, rubberlike substance, and put them on, drawing the long gauntlets up over his coat sleeves. Then he produced a bottle and unscrewed the cap. Being careful to avoid splashing his clothes, he went about, pouring a clear liquid upon the ground in several places. Where he poured, white vapors rose, and twigs and grass grumbled into brownish dust. After he had replaced the cap and returned the bottle to the bag, he waited for a few minutes, then took a spatula from the musette and dug where he had poured the fluid, prying loose four black, irregular-shaped lumps of matter, which he carried to the running water and washed carefully, before wrapping them and putting them in the bag, along with the gloves. Then he slung bag and rifle and started down the trail to where he had parked the jeep.

Half an hour later, after driving through the little farming village of Rutter's Fort, he pulled into the barnyard of a rundown farm and backed through the open doors of the barn. He closed the double doors behind him, and barred them from within. Then he went to the rear wall of the barn, which was much closer the front than the outside dimensions of the barn would have indicated.

He took from his pocket a black object like an automatic pencil. Hunting over the rough plank wall, he found a small hole and inserted the pointed end of the pseudo-pencil, pressing on the other end. For an instant, nothing happened. Then a ten-foot-square section of the wall receded two feet and slid noiselessly to one side. The section which had slid inward had been built of three-inch steel, masked by a thin covering of boards; the wall around it was two-foot concrete, similarly camouflaged. He stepped quickly inside.

Fumbling at the right side of the opening, he found a switch and flicked it. Instantly, the massive steel plate slid back into place with a soft, oily click. As it did, lights came on within the hidden room, disclosing a great semiglobe of some fine metallic mesh, thirty feet in diameter and fifteen in height. There was a sliding door at one side of this; the man called Richard Lee opened and entered through it, closing it behind him. Then he turned to the center of the hollow dome, where an armchair was placed in front of a small desk below a large instrument panel. The gauges and dials on the panel, and the levers and switches and buttons on the desk control board, were all lettered and numbered with characters not of the Roman alphabet or the Arabic notation, and, within instant reach of the occupant of the chair, a pistollike weapon lay on the desk. It had a conventional index-finger trigger and a hand-fit grip, but, instead of a tubular barrel, two slender parallel metal rods extended about four inches forward of the receiver, joined together at what would correspond to the muzzle by a streamlined knob of some light blue ceramic or plastic substance.

The man with the handsome immobile face deposited his rifle and musette on the floor beside the chair and sat down. First, he picked up the pistollike weapon and checked it, and then he examined the many instruments on the panel in front of him. Finally, he flicked a switch on the control board.

At once, a small humming began, from some point overhead. It wavered and shrilled and mounted in intensity, and then fell to a steady monotone. The dome about him flickered with a queer, cold iridescence, and slowly vanished. The hidden room vanished, and he was looking into the shadowy interior of a deserted barn. The barn vanished; blue sky appeared above, streaked with wisps of high cirrus cloud. The autumn landscape flickered unreally. Buildings appeared and vanished, and other buildings came and went in a twinkling. All around him, half-seen shapes moved briefly and disappeared.

Once, the figure of a man appeared, inside the circle of the dome. He had an angry, brutal face, and he wore a black tunic piped with silver, and black breeches, and polished black boots, and there was an insignia, composed of a cross and thunderbolt, on his cap. He held an automatic pistol in his hand.

Instantly, the man at the desk snatched up his own weapon and thumbed off the safety, but before he could lift and aim it, the intruder stumbled and passed outside the force-field which surrounded the chair and instruments.

For a while, there were fires raging outside, and for a while, the man at the desk was surrounded by a great hall, with a high, vaulted ceiling, through which figures flitted and vanished. For a while, there were vistas of deep forests, always set in the same background of mountains and always under the same blue cirrus-laced sky. There was an interval of flickering blue-white light, of unbearable intensity. Then the man at the desk was surrounded by the interior of vast industrial works. The moving figures around him slowed, and became more distinct. For an instant, the man in the chair grinned as he found himself looking into a big washroom, where a tall blond girl was taking a shower bath, and a pert little redhead was vigorously drying herself with a towel. The dome grew visible, coruscating with many-colored lights and then the humming died and the dome became a cold and inert mesh of fine white metal. A green light above flashed on and off slowly.

He stabbed a button and flipped a switch, then got to his feet, picking up his rifle and musette and fumbling under his shirt for a small mesh bag, from which he took an inch-wide disk of blue plastic. Unlocking a container on the instrument panel, he removed a small roll of solidograph-film, which he stowed in his bag. Then he slid open the door and emerged into his own dimension of space-time.

Outside was a wide hallway, with a pale green floor, paler green walls, and a ceiling of greenish off-white. A big hole had been cut to accommodate the dome, and across the hallway a desk had been set up, and at it sat a clerk in a pale blue tunic, who was just taking the audio-plugs of a music-box out of his ears. A couple of policemen in green uniforms, with ultrasonic paralyzers dangling by thongs from their left wrists and bolstered sigma-ray needlers like the one on the desk inside the dome, were kidding with some girls in vivid orange and scarlet and green smocks. One of these, in bright green, was a duplicate of the one he had seen rubbing herself down with a towel.

"Here comes your boss-man," one of the girls told the cops, as he approached. They both turned and saluted casually. The man who had lately been using the name of Richard Lee responded to their greeting and went to the desk. The policemen grasped their paralyzers, drew their needlers, and hurried into the dome.

Taking the disk of blue plastic from his packet, he handed it to the clerk at the desk, who dropped it into a slot in the voder in front of him. Instantly, a mechanical voice responded:

"Verkan Vall, blue-seal noble, hereditary Mavrad of Nerros. Special Chief's Assistant, Paratime Police, special assignment. Subject to no orders below those of Tortha Karf, Chief of Paratime Police. To be given all courtesies and cooperation within the Paratime Transposition Code and the Police Powers Code. Further particulars?"

The clerk pressed the "no"-button. The blue sigil fell out the release-slot and was handed back to its bearer, who was drawing up his left sleeve.

"You'll want to be sure I'm *your* Verkan Vall, I suppose?" he said, extending his arm.

"Yes, quite, sir."

The clerk touched his arm with a small instrument which swabbed it with antiseptic, drew a minute blood-sample, and medicated the needle prick, all in one almost painless operation. He put the blood-drop on a slide and inserted it at one side of a comparison microscope, nodding. It showed the same distinctive permanent colloid pattern as the sample he had ready for comparison; the colloid pattern given in infancy by injection to the man in front of him, to set him apart from all the myriad other Verkan Valls on every other probability-line of paratime.

"Right, sir," the clerk nodded.

The two policemen came out of the dome, their needlers holstered and their vigilance relaxed. They were lighting cigarettes as they emerged.

"It's all right, sir," one of them said. "You didn't bring anything in with you, this trip."

The other cop chuckled. "Remember that Fifth Level wild-man who came in on the freight conveyor at Jandar, last month?" he asked.

If he was hoping that some of the girls would want to know, what wild-man, it was a vain hope. With a blue-seal mavrad around, what chance did a couple of ordinary coppers have? The girls were already converging on Verkan Vall.

"When are you going to get that monstrosity out of our restroom," the little redhead in green coveralls was demanding. "If it wasn't for that thing, I'd be taking a shower, right now."

"You were just finishing one, about fifty paraseconds off, when I came through," Verkan Vall told her.

The girl looked at him in obviously feigned indignation.

"Why, you — You *parapeeper!*"

Verkan Vall chuckled and turned to the clerk. "I want a strato-rocket and pilot, for Dhergabar, right away. Call Dhergabar Paratime Police Field and give them my ETA; have an air-taxi meet me, and have the chief notified that I'm coming in. Extraordinary report. Keep a guard over the conveyor; I think I'm going to need it, again, soon." He turned to the little redhead. "Want to show me the way out of here, to the rocket field?" he asked.

Outside, on the open landing field, Verkan Vall glanced up at the sky, then looked at his watch. It had been twenty minutes since he had backed the jeep into the barn, on that distant other time-line; the same delicate lines of white cirrus were etched across the blue above. The constancy of the weather, even across two hundred thousand parayears of perpendicular time, never failed to impress him. The long curve of the mountains was the same, and they were mottled with the same autumn colors, but where the little village of Rutter's Fort stood on that other line of probability, the white towers of an apartment-city rose — the living quarters of the plant personnel.

The rocket that was to take him to headquarters was being hoisted with a crane and lowered into the firing-stand, and he walked briskly toward it, his rifle and musette slung. A boyish-looking pilot was on the platform, opening the door of the rocket; he stood aside for Verkan Vall to enter; then followed and closed it, dogging it shut while his passenger stowed his bag and rifle and strapped himself into a seat.

"Dhergabar Commercial Terminal, sir?" the pilot asked, taking the adjoining seat at the controls.

"Paratime Police Field, back of the Paratime Administration Building."

"Right, sir. Twenty seconds to blast, when you're ready."

"Ready now." Verkan Vall relaxed, counting seconds subconsciously.

The rocket trembled, and Verkan Vall felt himself being pushed gently back against the upholstery. The seats, and the pilot's instrument panel in front of them, swung on gimbals, and the finger of the indicator swept slowly over a ninety-degree arc as the rocket rose and leveled. By then, the high cirrus clouds Verkan Vall had watched from the field were far below; they were well into the stratosphere.

There would be nothing to do, now, for the three hours in which the rocket sped northward across the pole and southward to Dhergabar; the navigation was entirely in the electronic hands of the robot controls. Verkan Vall got out his pipe and lit it; the pilot lit a cigarette.

"That's an odd pipe, sir," the pilot said. "Out-time item?"

"Yes, Fourth Probability Level; typical of the whole paratime belt I was working in." Verkan Vall handed it over for inspection. "The bowl's natural brier-root; the stem's a sort of plastic made from the sap of certain tropical trees. The little white dot is the maker's trademark; it's made of elephant tusk."

"Sounds pretty crude to me, sir." The pilot handed it back. "Nice workmanship, though. Looks like good machine production."

"Yes. The sector I was on is really quite advanced, for an electro-chemical civilization. That weapon I brought back with me — that solid-missile projector — is typical of most Fourth Level culture. Moving parts machined to the closest tolerances, and interchangeable with similar parts of all similar weapons. The missile is a small bolt of cupro-alloy coated lead, propelled by expanding gases from the ignition of some nitro-cellulose compound. Most of their scientific advance occurred within the past century, and most of that in the past forty years. Of course, the life-expectancy on that level is only about seventy years."

"Humph! I'm seventy-eight, last birthday," the boyish-looking pilot snorted. "Their medical science must be mostly witchcraft!"

"Until quite recently, it was," Verkan Vall agreed. "Same story there as in everything else — rapid advancement in the past few decades, after thousands of years of cultural inertia."

"You know, sir, I don't really understand this paratime stuff," the pilot confessed. "I know that all time is totally present, and that every moment has its own past-future line of event-sequence, and that all events in space-time occur according to maximum probability, but I just don't get this alternate probability stuff, at all. If something exists, it's because it's the maximum-probability effect of prior causes; why does anything else exist on any other time-line?"

Verkan Vall blew smoke at the air-renovator. A lecture on paratime theory would nicely fill in the three-hour interval until the landing at Dhergabar. At least, this kid was asking intelligent questions.

"Well, you know the principal of time-passage, I suppose?" he began.

"Yes, of course; Rhogom's Doctrine. The basis of most of our psychical science. We exist perpetually at all moments within our life-span; our extraphysical ego component passes from the ego existing at one moment to the ego existing at the next. During unconsciousness, the EPC is 'time-free'; it may detach, and connect at some other moment, with the ego existing at that time-point. That's how we precog. We take an autohypno and recover memories brought back from the future moment and buried in the subconscious mind."

"That's right," Verkan Vall told him. "And even without the autohypno, a lot of precognitive matter leaks out of the subconscious and into the conscious mind, usually in distorted forms, or else inspires 'instinctive' acts, the motivation for which is not brought to the level of consciousness. For instance, suppose, you're walking along North Promenade, in Dhergabar, and you come to the Martian Palace Café, and you go in for a drink, and meet same girl, and strike up an acquaintance with her. This chance acquaintance develops into a love affair, and a year later, out of jealousy, she rays you half a dozen times with a needler."

"Just about that happened to a friend of mine, not long ago," the pilot said. "Go on, sir."

"Well, in the microsecond or so before you die — or afterward, for that matter, because we know that the extraphysical component survives physical destruction — your EPC slips back a couple of years, and re-connects at some point pastward of your first meeting with this girl, and carries with it memories of everything up to the moment of detachment, all of which are indelibly recorded in your subconscious mind. So, when you re-experience the event of standing outside the Martian Palace with a thirst, you go on to the Starway, or Nhergal's, or some other bar. In both cases, on both time-lines, you follow the line of maximum probability; in the second case, your subconscious future memories are an added causal factor."

"And when I back-slip, after I've been needled, I generate a new time-line? Is that it?"

Verkan Vall made a small sound of impatience. "No such thing!" he exclaimed. "It's semantically inadmissible to talk about the total presence of time with one breath and about generating new time-lines with the next. *All* time-lines are totally present, in perpetual co-existence. The theory is that the EPC passes from one moment, on one time-line, to the next moment on the next line, so that the true passage of the EPC from moment to moment is a two-dimensional diagonal. So, in the case we're using, the event of your going into the Martian Palace exists on one time-line, and the event of your passing along to the Starway exists on another, but both are events in real existence.

"Now, what we do, in paratime transposition, is to build up a hypertemporal field to include the time-line we want to reach, and then shift over to it. Same point in the plenum; same point in primary time — plus primary time elapsed during mechanical and electronic lag in the relays — but a different line of secondary time."

"Then why don't we have past-future time travel on our own time-line?" the pilot wanted to know.

That was a question every paratimer has to answer, every time he talks paratime to the laity. Verkan Vall had been expecting it; he answered patiently.

"The Ghaldron-Hesthor field-generator is like every other mechanism; it can operate only in the area of primary time in which it exists. It can transpose to any other time-line, and carry with it anything inside its field, but it can't go outside its own temporal area of existence, anymore than a bullet from that rifle can hit the target a week before it's fired," Verkan Vall pointed out. "Anything inside the field is supposed to be unaffected by anything outside. *Supposed to be* is the way to put it; it doesn't always work. Once in a while, something pretty nasty gets picked up in transit." He thought, briefly, of the man in the black tunic. "That's why we have armed guards at terminals."

"Suppose you pick up a blast from a nucleonic bomb," the pilot asked, "or something red-hot, or radioactive?"

"We have a monument, at Paratime Police Headquarters, in Dhergabar, bearing the names of our own personnel who didn't make it back. It's a large monument; over the past ten thousand years, it's been inscribed with quite a few names."

"You can have it; I'll stick to rockets!" the pilot replied. "Tell me another thing, though: What's all this about levels, and sectors, and belts? What's the difference?"

"Purely arbitrary terms. There are five main probability levels, derived from the five possible outcomes of the attempt to colonize this planet, seventy-five thousand years ago. We're on the First Level — complete success, and colony fully established. The Fifth Level is the probability of complete failure — no human population established on this planet, and indigenous quasi-human life evolved indigenously. On the Fourth Level, the colonists evidently met with some disaster and lost all memory of their extraterrestrial origin, as well as all extraterrestrial culture. As far as they know, they are an indigenous race; they have a long pre-history of stone-age savagery.

"Sectors are areas of paratime on any level in which the prevalent culture has a common origin and common characteristics. They are divided more or less arbitrarily into sub-sectors. Belts are areas within sub-sectors where conditions are the result of recent alternate probabilities. For instance, I've just come from the Europo-American Sector of the Fourth Level, an area of about ten thousand parayears in depth, in which the dominant civilization developed on the Northwest Continent of the Major Land Mass, and spread from there to the Minor Land Mass. The line on which I was operating is also part of a sub-sector of about three thousand parayears' depth, and a belt developing from one of several probable outcomes of a war concluded about three elapsed years ago. On that time-line, the field at the Hagraban Synthetics Works, where we took off, is part of an abandoned farm; on the site of Hagraban City is a little farming village. Those things are there, right now, both in primary time and in the plenum. They are about two hundred and fifty thousand parayears perpendicular to each other, and each is of the same general order of reality."

The red light overhead flashed on. The pilot looked into his visor and put his hands to the manual controls, in case of failure of the robot controls. The rocket landed smoothly, however; there was a slight jar as it was grappled by the crane and hoisted upright, the seats turning in their gimbals. Pilot and passenger unstrapped themselves and hurried through the refrigerated outlet and away from the glowing-hot rocket.

*A*n air-taxi, emblazoned with the device of the Paratime Police, was waiting. Verkan Vall said good-bye to the rocket-pilot and took his seat beside the pilot of the aircab; the latter lifted his vehicle above the building level and then set it down on the landing-stage of the Paratime Police Building in a long, side-swooping glide. An express elevator took Verkan Vall down to one of the middle stages, where he showed his sigil to the guard outside the door of Tortha Karf's office and was admitted at once.

The Paratime Police chief rose from behind his semicircular desk, with its array of keyboards and viewing-screens and communicators. He was a big man, well past his two hundredth year; his hair was iron-grey and thinning in front, he had begun to grow thick at the waist, and his calm features bore the lines of middle age. He wore the dark-green uniform of the Paratime Police.

"Well, Vall," he greeted. "Everything secure?"

"Not exactly, sir." Verkan Vall came around the desk, deposited his rifle and bag on the floor, and sat down in one of the spare chairs. "I'll have to go back again."

"So?" His chief lit a cigarette and waited.

"I traced Gavran Sarn." Verkan Vall got out his pipe and began to fill it. "But that's only the beginning. I have to trace something else. Gavran Sarn exceeded his Paratime permit, and took one of his pets along. A Venusian nighthound."

Tortha Karf's expression did not alter; it merely grew more intense. He used one of the short, semantically ugly terms which serve, in place of profanity, as the emotional release of a race that has forgotten all the taboos and terminologies of supernaturalistic religion and sex-inhibition.

"You're sure of this, of course." It was less a question than a statement.

Verkan Vall bent and took cloth-wrapped objects from his bag, unwrapping them and laying them on the desk. They were casts, in hard black plastic, of the footprints of some large three-toed animal.

"What do these look like, sir?" he asked.

Tortha Karf fingered them and nodded. Then he became as visibly angry as a man of his civilization and culture-level ever permitted himself.

"What does that fool think we have a Paratime Code for?" he demanded. "It's entirely illegal to transpose any extraterrestrial animal or object to any time-line on which space-travel is un-known. I don't care if he is a green-seal thavrad; he'll face charges, when he gets back, for this!"

"He *was* a green-seal thavrad," Verkan Vall corrected. "And he won't be coming back."

"I hope you didn't have to deal summarily with him," Tortha Karf said. "With his title, and social position, and his family's political importance, that might make difficulties. Not that it wouldn't be all right with me, of course, but we never seem to be able to make either the Management or the public realize the extremities to which we are forced, at times." He sighed. "We probably never shall."

Verkan Vall smiled faintly. "Oh, no, sir; nothing like that. He was dead before I transposed to that time-line. He was killed when he wrecked a self-propelled vehicle he was using. One of those

Fourth Level automobiles. I posed as a relative and tried to claim his body for the burial-ceremony observed on that cultural level, but was told that it had been completely destroyed by fire when the fuel tank of this automobile burned. I was given certain of his effects which had passed through the fire; I found his sigil concealed inside what appeared to be a cigarette case." He took a green disk from the bag and laid it on the desk. "There's no question; Gavran Sarn died in the wreck of that automobile."

"And the nighthound?"

"It was in the car with him, but it escaped. You know how fast those things are. I found that track" — he indicated one of the black casts — "in some dried mud near the scene of the wreck. As you see, the cast is slightly defective. The others were fresh this morning, when I made them."

"And what have you done so far?"

"I rented an old farm near the scene of the wreck, and installed my field-generator there. It runs through to the Hagraban Synthetics Works, about a hundred miles east of Thalna-Jarvizar. I have my this-line terminal in the girls' rest room at the durable plastics factory; handled that on a local police-power writ. Since then, I've been hunting for the nighthound. I think I can find it, but I'll need some special equipment, and a hypno-mech indoctrination. That's why I came back."

"Has it been attracting any attention?" Tortha Karf asked anxiously.

"Killing cattle in the locality; causing considerable excitement. Fortunately, it's a locality of forested mountains and valley farms, rather than a built-up industrial district. Local police and wild-game protection officers are concerned; all the farmers excited, and going armed. The theory is that it's either a wildcat of some sort, or a maniac armed with a cutlass. Either theory would conform, more or less, to the nature of its depredations. Nobody has actually seen it."

"That's good!" Tortha Karf was relieved. "Well, you'll have to go and bring it out, or kill it and obliterate the body. You know why, as well as I do."

"Certainly, sir," Verkan Vall replied. "In a primitive culture, things like this would be assigned supernatural explanations, and imbedded in the locally accepted religion. But this culture, while nominally religious, is highly rationalistic in practice. Typical lag-effect, characteristic of all expanding cultures. And this Europo-American Sector really has an expanding culture. A hundred and fifty years ago, the inhabitants of this particular time-line didn't even know how to apply steam power; now they've begun to release nuclear energy, in a few crude forms."

Tortha Karf whistled, softly. "That's quite a jump. There's a sector that'll be in for trouble, in the next few centuries."

"That is realized, locally, sir." Verkan Vall concentrated on relighting his pipe, for a moment, then continued: "I would predict space-travel on that sector within the next century. Maybe the next half-century, at least to the Moon. And the art of taxidermy is very highly developed. Now, suppose some farmer shoots that thing; what would he do with it, sir?"

Tortha Karf grunted. "Nice logic, Vall. On a most uncomfortable possibility. He'd have it mounted, and it'd be put in a museum, somewhere. And as soon as the first spaceship reaches Venus, and they find those things in a wild state, they'll have the mounted specimen identified."

"Exactly. And then, instead of beating their brains about *where* their specimen came from, they'll begin asking *when* it came from. They're quite capable of such reasoning, even now."

"A hundred years isn't a particularly long time," Tortha Karf considered. "I'll be retired, then, but you'll have my job, and it'll be your headache. You'd better get this cleaned up, now, while it can be handled. What are you going to do?"

"I'm not sure, now, sir. I want a hypno-mech indoctrination, first." Verkan Vall gestured toward the communicator on the desk. "May I?" he asked.

"Certainly." Tortha Karf slid the instrument across the desk. "Anything you want."

"Thank you, sir." Verkan Vall snapped on the code-index, found the symbol he wanted, and then punched it on the keyboard. "Special Chief's Assistant Verkan Vall," he identified himself. "Speaking from office of Tortha Karf, Chief Paratime Police. I want a complete hypno-mech on Venusian nighthounds, emphasis on wild state, special emphasis domesticated nighthounds reverted to wild state in terrestrial surroundings, extra-special emphasis hunting techniques applicable to same. The word 'nighthound' will do for trigger-symbol." He turned to Tortha Karf. "Can I take it here?"

Tortha Karf nodded, pointing to a row of booths along the far wall of the office.

"Make set-up for wired transmission; I'll take it here."

"Very well, sir; in fifteen minutes," a voice replied out of the communicator.

Verkan Vall slid the communicator back. "By the way, sir; I had a hitchhiker, on the way back. Carried him about a hundred or so parayears; picked him up about three hundred parayears after leaving my other-line terminal. Nasty-looking fellow, in a black uniform; looked like one of these private-army storm troopers you find all through that sector. Armed, and hostile. I thought I'd have to ray him, but he blundered outside the field almost at once. I have a record, if you'd care to see it."

"Yes, put it on," Tortha Karf gestured toward the solidograph-projector. "It's set for miniature reproduction here on the desk; that be all right?"

Verkan Vall nodded, getting out the film and loading it into the projector. When he pressed a button, a dome of radiance appeared on the desk top; two feet in width and a foot in height. In the middle of this appeared a small solidograph image of the interior of the conveyor, showing the desk, and the control board, and the figure of Verkan Vall seated at it. The little figure of the storm trooper appeared, pistol in hand. The little Verkan Vall snatched up his tiny needler; the storm trooper moved into one side of the dome and vanished.

Verkan Vall flipped a switch and cut out the image.

"Yes. I don't know what causes that, but it happens, now and then," Tortha Karf said. "Usually at the beginning of a transposition. I remember, when I was just a kid, about a hundred and fifty years ago — a hundred and thirty-nine, to be exact — I picked up a fellow on the Fourth Level, just about where you're operating, and dragged him a couple of hundred parayears. I went back to find him and return him to his own time-line, but before I could locate him, he'd been arrested by the local authorities as a suspicious character, and got himself shot trying to escape. I felt badly about that, but —" Tortha Karf shrugged. "Anything else happen on the trip?"

"I ran through a belt of intermittent nucleonic bombing on the Second Level." Verkan Vall mentioned an approximate paratime location.

"Aaagh! That Khiftan civilization — by courtesy so called!" Tortha Karf pulled a wry face. "I suppose the intra-family enmities of the Hvadka Dynasty have reached critical mass again. They'll fool around till they blast themselves back to the stone age."

"Intellectually, they're about there, now. I had to operate in that sector, once — Oh, yes, another thing, sir. This rifle." Verkan Vall picked it up, emptied the magazine, and handed it to his superior. "The supplies office slipped up on this; it's not appropriate to my line of operation. It's a lovely rifle, but it's about two hundred percent in advance of existing arms design on my line. It excited the curiosity of a couple of police officers and a game-protector, who should be familiar with the weapons of their own time-line. I evaded by disclaiming ownership or intimate knowledge, and they seemed satisfied, but it worried me."

"Yes. That was made in our duplicating shops, here in Dhergabar." Tortha Karf carried it to a photographic bench, behind his desk. "I'll have it checked, while you're taking your hypno-mech. Want to exchange it for something authentic?"

"Why, no, sir. It's been identified to me, and I'd excite less suspicion with it than I would if I abandoned it and mysteriously acquired another rifle. I just wanted a check, and Supplies warned to be more careful in future."

Tortha Karf nodded approvingly. The young Mavrad of Nerros was thinking as a paratimer should.

"What's the designation of your line, again?"

Verkan Vall told him. It was a short numerical term of six places, but it expressed a number of the order of ten to the fortieth power, exact to the last digit. Tortha Karf repeated it into his stenomemograph, with explanatory comment.

"There seems to be quite a few things going wrong, in that area," he said. "Let's see, now."

He punched the designation on a keyboard; instantly, it appeared on a translucent screen in front of him. He punched another combination, and, at the top of the screen, under the number, there appeared:

EVENTS, PAST ELAPSED FIVE YEARS.

He punched again; below this line appeared the sub-heading:

EVENTS INVOLVING PARATIME TRANSPOSITION.

Another code-combination added a third line:

(ATTRACTING PUBLIC NOTICE AMONG INHABITANTS.)

He pressed the "start"-button; the headings vanished, to be replaced by page after page of print, succeeding one another on the screen as the two men read. They told strange and apparently disconnected stories — of unexplained fires and explosions; of people vanishing without trace; of unaccountable disasters to aircraft. There were many stories of an epidemic of mysterious disk-shaped objects seen in the sky, singly or in numbers. To each account was appended one or more reference-numbers. Sometimes Tortha Karf or Verkan Vall would punch one of these, and read, on an adjoining screen, the explanatory matter referred to.

Finally Tortha Karf leaned back and lit a fresh cigarette.

"Yes, indeed, Vall; very definitely we will have to take action in the matter of the runaway nighthound of the late Gavran Sarn," he said. "I'd forgotten that that was the time-line onto which the *Ardrath* expedition launched those antigrav disks. If this extraterrestrial monstrosity turns up, on the heels of that 'Flying Saucer' business, everybody above the order of intelligence of a cretin will suspect some connection."

"What really happened, in the *Ardrath* matter?" Verkan Vall inquired. "I was on the Third Level, on that Luvarian Empire operation, at the time."

"That's right; you missed that. Well, it was one of these joint-operation things. The Paratime Commission and the Space Patrol were experimenting with a new technique for throwing a spaceship into paratime. They used the cruiser *Ardrath*, Kalzarn Jann commanding. Went into space about halfway to the Moon and took up orbit, keeping on the sunlit side of the planet to avoid being observed. That was all right. But then, Captain Kalzarn ordered away a flight of antigrav disks, fully manned, to take pictures, and finally authorized a landing in the western mountain range, Northern Continent, Minor Land-Mass. That's when the trouble started."

He flipped the run-back switch, till he had recovered the page he wanted. Verkan Vall read of a Fourth Level aviator, in his little airscrew-drive craft, sighting nine high-flying saucerlike objects.

"That was how it began," Tortha Karf told him. "Before long, as other incidents of the same sort occurred, our people on that line began sending back to know what was going on. Naturally, from the different descriptions of these 'saucers,' they recognized the objects as antigrav landing-disks from a spaceship. So I went to the Commission and raised atomic blazes about it, and the *Ardrath* was ordered to confine operations to the lower areas of the Fifth Level. Then our people on that time-line went to work with corrective action. Here."

He wiped the screen and then began punching combinations. Page after page appeared, bearing accounts of people who had claimed to have seen the mysterious disks, and each report was more fantastic than the last.

"The standard smother-out technique," Verkan Vall grinned. "I only heard a little talk about the 'Flying Saucers,' and all of that was in joke. In that order of culture, you can always discredit one true story by setting up ten others, palpably false, parallel to it — Wasn't that the time-line the Tharmax Trading Corporation almost lost their paratime license on?"

"That's right; it was! They bought up all the cigarettes, and caused a conspicuous shortage, after Fourth Level cigarettes had been introduced on this line and had become popular. They should have spread their purchases over a number of lines, and kept them within the local supply-demand frame. And they also got into trouble with the local government for selling unrationed petrol and automobile tires. We had to send in a special-operations group, and they came closer to having to engage in out-time local politics than I care to think of." Tortha Karf quoted a line from a currently popular song about the sorrows of a policeman's life. "We're jugglers, Vall; trying to keep our traders and sociological observers and tourists and plain idiots like the late Gavran Sarn out of trouble; trying to prevent panics and disturbances and dislocations of local economy as a result of our operations; trying to keep out of out-time politics — and, at all times, at all costs and hazards, by all means, guarding the secret of paratime transposition. Sometimes I wish Ghaldron Karf and Hesthor Ghrom had strangled in their cradles!"

Verkan Vall shook his head. "No, chief," he said. "You don't mean that; not really," he said. "We've been paratiming for the past ten thousand years. When the Ghaldron-Hesthor trans-temporal field was discovered, our ancestors had pretty well exhausted the resources of this planet. We had a world population of half a billion, and it was all they could do to keep alive. After we began paratime transposition, our population climbed to ten billion, and there it stayed for the last eight thousand years. Just enough of us to enjoy our planet and the other planets of the system to the fullest; enough of everything for everybody that nobody needs fight anybody for anything. We've tapped the resources of those other worlds on other time-lines, a little here, a little there, and not enough to really hurt anybody. We've left our mark in a few places — the Dakota Badlands, and the Gobi, on the Fourth Level, for instance — but we've done no great damage to any of them."

"Except the time they blew up half the Southern Island Continent, over about five hundred parayears on the Third Level," Tortha Karf mentioned.

"Regrettable accident, to be sure," Verkan Vall conceded. "And look how much we've learned from the experiences of those other time-lines. During the Crisis, after the Fourth Interplanetary War, we might have adopted Palnar Sarn's 'Dictatorship of the Chosen' scheme, if we hadn't seen what an exactly similar scheme had done to the Jak-Hakka Civilization, on the Second Level. When Palnar Sarn was told about that, he went into paratime to see for himself, and when he returned, he renounced his proposal in horror."

Tortha Karf nodded. He wouldn't be making any mistake in turning his post over to the Mavrad of Nerros on his retirement.

"Yes, Vall; I know," he said. "But when you've been at this desk as long as I have, you'll have a sour moment or two, now and then, too."

A blue light flashed over one of the booths across the room. Verkan Vall got to his feet, removing his coat and hanging it on the back of his chair, and crossed the room, rolling up his left shirt sleeve. There was a relaxer-chair in the booth, with a blue plastic helmet above it. He glanced at the indicator-screen to make sure he was getting the indoctrination he called for, and then sat down in the chair and lowered the helmet over his head, inserting the ear plugs and fastening the chin strap. Then he touched his left arm with an injector which was lying on the arm of the chair, and at the same time flipped the starter switch.

Soft, slow music began to chant out of the earphones. The insidious fingers of the drug blocked off his senses, one by one. The music diminished, and the words of the hypnotic formula lulled him to sleep.

He woke, hearing the lively strains of dance music. For a while, he lay relaxed. Then he snapped off the switch, took out the ear plugs, removed the helmet and rose to his feet. Deep in his subconscious mind was the entire body of knowledge about the Venusian nighthound. He mentally pronounced the word, and at once it began flooding into his conscious mind. He knew the animal's evolutionary history, its anatomy, its characteristics, its dietary and reproductive habits, how it hunted, how it fought its enemies, how it eluded pursuit, and how best it could be tracked down and killed. He nodded. Already, a plan for dealing with Gavran Sarn's renegade pet was taking shape in his mind.

He picked a plastic cup from the dispenser, filled it from a cooler-tap with amber-colored spiced wine, and drank, tossing the cup into the disposal-bin. He placed a fresh injector on the arm of the chair, ready for the next user of the booth. Then he emerged, glancing at his Fourth Level wrist watch and mentally translating to the First Level time-scale. Three hours had passed; there had been more to learn about his quarry than he had expected.

Tortha Karf was sitting behind his desk, smoking a cigarette. It seemed as though he had not moved since Verkan Vall had left him, though the special agent knew that he had dined, attended several conferences, and done many other things.

"I checked up on your hitchhiker, Vall," the chief said. "We won't bother about him. He's a member of something called the Christian Avengers — one of those typical Europo-American race-and-religious hate groups. He belongs in a belt that is the outcome of the Hitler victory of 1940, whatever that was. Something unpleasant, I daresay. We don't owe him anything; people of that sort should be stepped on, like cockroaches. And he won't make anymore trouble on the line where you dropped him than they have there already. It's in a belt of complete social and political anarchy; somebody probably shot him as soon as he emerged, because he wasn't wearing the right sort of a uniform. Nineteen-forty what, by the way?"

"Elapsed years since the birth of some religious leader," Verkan Vall explained. "And did you find out about my rifle?"

"Oh, yes. It's reproduction of something that's called a Sharp's Model '37 .235 Ultraspeed-Express. Made on an adjoining para-time belt by a company that went out of business sixty-seven years ago, elapsed time, on your line of operation. What made the difference was the Second War Between The States. I don't know what that was, either — I'm not too well up on Fourth Level history — but whatever, your line of operation didn't have it. Probably just as well for them, though they very likely had something else, as bad or worse. I put in a complaint to Supplies about it, and got you some more ammunition and reloading tools. Now, tell me what you're going to do about this nighthound business."

Tortha Karf was silent for a while, after Verkan Vall had finished.

"You're taking some awful chances, Vall," he said, at length. "The way you plan doing it, the advantages will all be with the nighthound. Those things can see as well at night as you can in daylight. I suppose you know that, though; you're the nighthound specialist, now."

"Yes. But they're accustomed to the Venus hotland marshes; it's been dry weather for the last two weeks, all over the northeastern section of the Northern Continent. I'll be able to hear it, long before it gets close to me. And I'll be wearing an electric headlamp. When I snap that on, it'll be dazzled, for a moment."

"Well, as I said, you're the nighthound specialist. There's the communicator; order anything you need." He lit a fresh cigarette from the end of the old one before crushing it out. "But be careful, Vall. It took me close to forty years to make a paratimer out of you; I don't want to have to repeat the process with somebody else before I can retire."

*T*he grass was wet as Verkan Vall — who reminded himself that here he was called Richard Lee — crossed the yard from the farmhouse to the ramshackle barn, in the early autumn darkness. It had been raining that morning when the strato-rocket from Dhergabar had landed him at the Hagraban Synthetics Works, on the First Level; unaffected by the probabilities of human history, the same rain had been coming down on the old Kinchwalter farm, near Rutter's Fort, on the Fourth Level. And it had persisted all day, in a slow, deliberate drizzle.

He didn't like that. The woods would be wet, muffling his quarry's footsteps, and canceling his only advantage over the night-prowler he hunted. He had no idea, however, of postponing the hunt. If anything, the rain had made it all the more imperative that the nighthound be killed at once. At this season, a falling temperature would speedily follow. The nighthound, a creature of the hot Venus marshes, would suffer from the cold, and, taught by years of domestication to find warmth among human habitations, it would invade some isolated farmhouse, or, worse, one of the little valley villages. If it were not killed tonight, the incident he had come to prevent would certainly occur.

Going to the barn, he spread an old horse blanket on the seat of the jeep, laid his rifle on it, and then backed the jeep outside. Then he took off his coat, removing his pipe and tobacco from the pockets, and spread it on the wet grass. He unwrapped a package and took out a small plastic spray-gun he had brought with him from the First Level, aiming it at the coat and pressing the trigger until it blew itself empty. A sickening, rancid fetor tainted the air — the scent of the giant poison-roach of Venus, the one creature for which the nighthound bore an inborn, implacable hatred. It was because of this compulsive urge to attack and kill the deadly poison-roach that the first human settlers on Venus, long millennia ago, had domesticated the ugly and savage nighthound. He remembered that the Gavran family derived their title from their vast Venus hotlands estates; that Gavran Sarn, the man who had brought this thing to the Fourth Level, had been born on the inner planet. When Verkan Vall donned that coat, he would become his own living bait for the murderous fury of the creature he sought. At the moment, mastering his queasiness and putting on the coat, he objected less to that danger than to the hideous stench of the scent, to obtain which a valuable specimen had been sacrificed at the Dhergabar Museum of Extraterrestrial Zoology, the evening before.

Carrying the wrapper and the spray-gun to an outside fireplace, he snapped his lighter to them and tossed them in. They were highly inflammable, blazing up and vanishing in a moment. He tested the electric headlamp on the front of his cap; checked his rifle; drew the heavy revolver, an authentic product of his line of operation, and flipped the cylinder out and in again. Then he got into the jeep and drove away.

For half an hour, he drove quickly along the valley roads. Now and then, he passed farmhouses, and dogs, puzzled and angered by the alien scent his coat bore, barked furiously. At length, he turned into a back road, and from this to the barely discernible trace of an old log road. The rain had stopped, and, in order to be ready to fire in any direction at any time, he had removed the top of the jeep. Now he had to crouch below the windshield to avoid overhanging branches. Once three deer — a buck and two does — stopped in front of him and stared for a moment, then bounded away with a flutter of white tails.

He was driving slowly, now; laying behind him a reeking trail of scent. There had been another stock-killing, the night before, while he had been on the First Level. The locality of this latest depredation had confirmed his estimate of the beast's probable movements, and indicated where it might be prowling, tonight. He was certain that it was somewhere near; sooner or later, it would pick up the scent.

Finally, he stopped, snapping out his lights. He had chosen this spot carefully, while studying the Geological Survey map, that afternoon; he was on the grade of an old railroad line, now abandoned and its track long removed, which had served the logging operations of fifty years ago. On one side, the mountain slanted sharply upward; on the other, it fell away sharply. If the nighthound were below him, it would have to climb that forty-five degree slope, and could not avoid dislodging loose stones, or otherwise making a noise. He would get out on that side; if the nighthound were above him, the jeep would protect him when it charged. He got to the ground, thumbing off the safety of his rifle, and an instant later he knew that he had made a mistake which could easily cost him his life; a mistake from which neither his comprehensive logic nor his hypnotically acquired knowledge of the beast's habits had saved him.

As he stepped to the ground, facing toward the front of the jeep, he heard a low, whining cry behind him, and a rush of padded feet. He whirled, snapping on the headlamp with his left hand and thrusting out his rifle pistol-wise in his right. For a split second, he saw the charging animal, its long, lizardlike head split in a toothy grin, its talon-tipped fore-paws extended.

He fired, and the bullet went wild. The next instant, the rifle was knocked from his hand. Instinctively, he flung up his left arm to shield his eyes. Claws raked his left arm and shoulder, something struck him heavily along the left side, and his cap-light went out as he dropped and rolled under the jeep, drawing in his legs and fumbling under his coat for the revolver.

In that instant, he knew what had gone wrong. His plan had been entirely too much of a success. The nighthound had winded him as he had driven up the old railroad-grade, and had followed. Its best running speed had been just good enough to keep it a hundred or so feet behind the jeep, and the motor-noise had covered the padding of its feet. In the few moments between stopping the little car and getting out, the nighthound had been able to close the distance and spring upon him.

It was characteristic of First-Level mentality that Verkan Vall wasted no moments on self-reproach or panic. While he was still rolling under his jeep, his mind had been busy with plans to retrieve the situation. Something touched the heel of one boot, and he froze his leg into immobility, at the same time trying to get the big Smith & Wesson free. The shoulder-holster, he found, was badly torn, though made of the heaviest skirting-leather, and the spring which retained the weapon in place had been wrenched and bent until he needed both hands to draw. The eight-inch slashing-claw of the nighthound's right intermediary limb had raked him; only the instinctive motion of throwing up his arm, and the fact that he wore the revolver in a shoulder-holster, had saved his life.

The nighthound was prowling around the jeep, whining frantically. It was badly confused. It could see quite well, even in the close darkness of the starless night; its eyes were of a nature capable of perceiving infrared radiations as light. There were plenty of these; the jeep's engine, lately running on four-wheel drive, was quite hot. Had he been standing alone, especially on this raw, chilly

night, Verkan Vall's own body-heat would have lighted him up like
a jack-o'-lantern. Now, however, the hot engine above him masked
his own radiations. Moreover, the poison-roach scent on his coat
was coming up through the floor board and mingling with the
scent on the seat, yet the nighthound couldn't find the two-and-
a-half foot insectlike thing that should have been producing it.
Verkan Vall lay motionless, wondering how long the next move
would be in coming. Then he heard a thud above him, followed
by a furious tearing as the nighthound ripped the blanket and
began rending at the seat cushion.

"Hope it gets a paw-full of seat-springs," Verkan Vall commented
mentally. He had already found a stone about the size of his two
fists, and another slightly smaller, and had put one in each of the
side pockets of the coat. Now he slipped his revolver into his
waist-belt and writhed out of the coat, shedding the ruined shoulder-holster at the same time. Wriggling on the flat of his back, he
squirmed between the rear wheels, until he was able to sit up,
behind the jeep. Then, swinging the weighted coat, he flung it
forward, over the nighthound and the jeep itself, at the same time
drawing his revolver.

Immediately, the nighthound, lured by the sudden movement
of the principal source of the scent, jumped out of the jeep and
bounded after the coat, and there was considerable noise in the
brush on the lower side of the railroad grade. At once, Verkan Vall
swarmed into the jeep and snapped on the lights.

His stratagem had succeeded beautifully. The stinking coat had
landed on the top of a small bush, about ten feet in front of the
jeep and ten feet from the ground. The nighthound, erect on its
haunches, was reaching out with its front paws to drag it down,
and slashing angrily at it with its single-clawed intermediary limbs.
Its back was to Verkan Vall.

His sights clearly defined by the lights in front of him, the
paratimer centered them on the base of the creature's spine, just
above its secondary shoulders, and carefully squeezed the trigger.
The big .357 Magnum bucked in his hand and belched flame and
sound — if only these Fourth Level weapons weren't so confound-
edly boisterous! — and the nighthound screamed and fell. Recock-
ing the revolver, Verkan Vall waited for an instant, then nodded
in satisfaction. The beast's spine had been smashed, and its hind
quarters, and even its intermediary fighting limbs had been para-
lyzed. He aimed carefully for a second shot and fired into the base
of the thing's skull. It quivered and died.

Getting a flashlight, he found his rifle, sticking muzzle-down in the mud a little behind and to the right of the jeep, and swore briefly in the local Fourth Level idiom, for Verkan Vall was a man who loved good weapons, be they sigma-ray needlers, neutron-disruption blasters, or the solid-missile projectors of the lower levels. By this time, he was feeling considerable pain from the claw-wounds he had received. He peeled off his shirt and tossed it over the hood of the jeep.

Tortha Karf had advised him to carry a needler, or a blaster, or a neurostat-gun, but Verkan Vall had been unwilling to take such arms onto the Fourth Level. In event of mishap to himself, it would be all too easy for such a weapon to fall into the hands of someone able to deduce from it scientific principles too far in advance of the general Fourth Level culture. But there had been one First Level item which he had permitted himself, mainly because, suitably packaged, it was not readily identifiable as such. Digging a respectable Fourth-Level leatherette case from under the seat, he opened it and took out a pint bottle with a red poison-label, and a towel. Saturating the towel with the contents of the bottle, he rubbed every inch of his torso with it, so as not to miss even the smallest break made in his skin by the septic claws of the nighthound. Whenever the lotion-soaked towel touched raw skin, a pain like the burn of a hot iron shot through him; before he was through, he was in agony. Satisfied that he had disinfected every wound, he dropped the towel and clung weakly to the side of the jeep. He grunted out a string of English oaths, and capped them with an obscene Spanish blasphemy he had picked up among the Fourth Level inhabitants of his island home of Nerros, to the south, and a thundering curse in the name of Mogga, Fire-God of Dool, in a Third-Level tongue. He mentioned Fasif, Great God of Khift, in a manner which would have got him an acid-bath if the Khiftan priests had heard him. He alluded to the baroque amatory practices of the Third-Level Illyalla people, and soothed himself, in the classical Dar-Halma tongue, with one of those rambling genealogical insults favored in the Indo-Turanian Sector of the Fourth Level.

By this time, the pain had subsided to an overall smarting itch. He'd have to bear with that until his work was finished and he could enjoy a hot bath. He got another bottle out of the first-aid kit — a flat pint, labeled "Old Overholt," containing a locally-manufactured specific for inward and subjective wounds — and medicated himself copiously from it, corking it and slipping it into his hip pocket against future need. He gathered up the ruined shoulder-holster and threw it under the back seat. He put on his shirt. Then he went and dragged the dead nighthound onto the grade by its stumpy tail.

It was an ugly thing, weighing close to two hundred pounds, with powerfully muscled hind legs which furnished the bulk of its motive-power, and sturdy three-clawed front legs. Its secondary limbs, about a third of the way back from its front shoulders, were long and slender; normally, they were carried folded closely against the body, and each was armed with a single curving claw. The revolver-bullet had gone in at the base of the skull and emerged under the jaw; the head was relatively undamaged. Verkan Vall was glad of that; he wanted that head for the trophy-room of his home on Nerros. Grunting and straining, he got the thing into the back of the jeep, and flung his almost shredded tweed coat over it.

A last look around assured him that he had left nothing unaccountable or suspicious. The brush was broken where the nighthound had been tearing at the coat; a bear might have done that. There were splashes of the viscid stuff the thing had used for blood, but they wouldn't be there long. Terrestrial rodents liked nighthound blood, and the woods were full of mice. He climbed in under the wheel, backed, turned, and drove away.

*I*nside the paratime-transposition dome, Verkan Vall turned from the body of the nighthound, which he had just dragged in, and considered the inert form of another animal — a stump-tailed, tuft-eared, tawny Canada lynx. That particular animal had already made two paratime transpositions; captured in the vast wilderness of Fifth-Level North America, it had been taken to the First Level and placed in the Dhergabar Zoological Gardens, and then, requisitioned on the authority of Tortha Karf, it had been brought to the Fourth Level by Verkan Vall. It was almost at the end of all its travels.

Verkan Vall prodded the supine animal with the toe of his boot; it twitched slightly. Its feet were cross-bound with straps, but when he saw that the narcotic was wearing off, Verkan Vall snatched a syringe, parted the fur at the base of its neck, and gave it an injection. After a moment, he picked it up in his arms and carried it out to the jeep.

"All right, pussy cat," he said, placing it under the rear seat, "this is the one-way ride. The way you're doped up, it won't hurt a bit."

He went back and rummaged in the debris of the long-deserted barn. He picked up a hoe, and discarded it as too light. An old plowshare was too unhandy. He considered a grate-bar from a heating furnace, and then he found the poleax, lying among a pile of wormeaten boards. Its handle had been shortened, at some time, to about twelve inches, converting it into a heavy hatchet. He weighed it, and tried it on a block of wood, and then, making sure that the secret door was closed, he went out again and drove off.

An hour later, he returned. Opening the secret door, he carried the ruined shoulder holster, and the straps that had bound the bobcat's feet, and the ax, now splotched with blood and tawny cat-hairs, into the dome. Then he closed the secret room, and took a long drink from the bottle on his hip.

The job was done. He would take a hot bath, and sleep in the farmhouse till noon, and then he would return to the First Level. Maybe Tortha Karf would want him to come back here for a while. The situation on this time-line was far from satisfactory, even if the crisis threatened by Gavran Sarn's renegade pet had been averted. The presence of a chief's assistant might be desirable.

At least, he had a right to expect a short vacation. He thought of the little redhead at the Hagraban Synthetics Works. What was her name? Something Kara — Morvan Kara; that was it. She'd be coming off shift about the time he'd make First Level, tomorrow afternoon.

The claw-wounds were still smarting vexatiously. A hot bath, and a night's sleep — He took another drink, lit his pipe, picked up his rifle and started across the yard to the house.

*P*rivate Zinkowski cradled the telephone and got up from the desk, stretching. He left the orderly-room and walked across the hall to the recreation room, where the rest of the boys were loafing. Sergeant Haines, in a languid gin-rummy game with Corporal Conner, a sheriff's deputy, and a mechanic from the service station down the road, looked up.

"Well, Sarge, I think we can write off those stock-killings," the private said.

"Yeah?" The sergeant's interest quickened.

"Yeah. I think the whatzit's had it. I just got a buzz from the railroad cops at Logansport. It seems a track-walker found a dead bobcat on the Logan River branch, about a mile or so below MMY signal tower. Looks like it tangled with that night freight up-river, and came off second best. It was near chopped to hamburger."

"MMY signal tower; that's right below Yoder's Crossing," the sergeant considered. "The Strawmyer farm night-before-last, the Amrine farm last night — Yeah, that would be about right."

"That'll suit Steve Parker; bobcats aren't protected, so it's not his trouble. And they're not a violation of state law, so it's none of our worry," Conner said. "Your deal, isn't it, Sarge?"

"Yeah. Wait a minute." The sergeant got to his feet. "I promised Sam Kane, the AP man at Logansport, that I'd let him in on anything new." He got up and started for the phone. "Phantom Killer!" He blew an impolite noise.

"Well, it was a lot of excitement, while it lasted," the deputy sheriff said. "Just like that Flying Saucer thing."

Naudsonce

*T*he sun warmed Mark Howell's back pleasantly. Underfoot, the mosslike stuff was soft and yielding, and there was a fragrance in the air unlike anything he had ever smelled. He was going to like this planet; he knew it. The question was, how would it, and its people, like him? He watched the little figures advancing across the fields from the mound, with the village out of sight on the other end of it and the combat-car circling lazily on contragravity above.

Major Luis Gofredo, the Marine officer, spoke without lowering his binoculars:

"They have a tubular thing about twelve feet long; six of them are carrying it on poles, three to a side, and a couple more are walking behind it. Mark, do you think it could be a cannon?"

So far, he didn't know enough to have an opinion, and said so, adding:

"What I saw of the village in the screen from the car, it looked pretty primitive. Of course, gunpowder's one of those things a primitive people could discover by accident, if the ingredients were available."

"We won't take any chances, then."

"You think they're hostile? I was hoping they were coming out to parley with us."

That was Paul Meillard. He had a right to be anxious; his whole future in the Colonial Office would be made or ruined by what was going to happen here.

The joint Space Navy-Colonial Office expedition was looking for new planets suitable for colonization; they had been out, now, for four years, which was close to maximum for an exploring expedition. They had entered eleven systems, and made landings on eight planets. Three had been reasonably close to Terra-type. There had been Fafnir; conditions there would correspond to Terra during the Cretaceous Period, but any Cretaceous dinosaur would

have been cute and cuddly to the things on Fafnir. Then there had
been Imhotep; in twenty or thirty thousand years, it would be a
fine planet, but at present it was undergoing an extensive glacia-
tion. And Irminsul, covered with forests of gigantic trees; it would
have been fine except for the fauna, which was nasty, especially a
race of subsapient near-humanoids who had just gotten as far as
clubs and *coup-de-poing* axes. Contact with them had entailed heavy
ammunition expenditure, with two men and a woman killed and
a dozen injured. He'd had a limp, himself, for a while as a result.

As for the other five, one had been an all-out hell-planet, and
the rest had been the sort that get colonized by irreconcilable
minority-groups who want to get away from everybody else. The
Colonial Office wouldn't even consider any of them.

Then they had found this one, third of a GO-star, eighty million
miles from primary, less axial inclination than Terra, which would
mean a more uniform year-round temperature, and about half land
surface. On the evidence of a couple of sneak landings for specimens, the biochemistry was identical with Terra's and the organic
matter was edible. It was the sort of planet every explorer dreams
of finding, except for one thing.

It was inhabited by a sapient humanoid race, and some of them
were civilized enough to put it in Class V, and Colonial Office
doctrine on Class V planets was rigid. Friendly relations with the
natives had to be established, and permission to settle had to be
guaranteed in a treaty of some sort with somebody more or less
authorized to make one.

If Paul Meillard could accomplish that, he had it made. He
would stay on with forty or fifty of the ship's company to make
preparations. In a year a couple of ships would come out from
Terra, with a thousand colonists, and a battalion or so of Federation troops, to protect them from the natives and vice versa.
Meillard would automatically be appointed governor-general.

But if he failed, he was through. Not out — just through. When
he got back to Terra, he would be promoted to some home office
position at slightly higher base pay but without the three hundred
percent extraterrestrial bonus, and he would vegetate there till he
retired. Every time his name came up, somebody would say, "Oh,
yes; he flubbed the contact on Whatzit."

It wouldn't do the rest of them any good, either. There would
always be the suspicion that they had contributed to the failure.

Bwaaa-waaa-waaanh!

The wavering sound hung for an instant in the air. A few
seconds later, it was repeated, then repeated again.

"Our cannon's a horn," Gofredo said. "I can't see how they're blowing it, though."

There was a stir to right and left, among the Marines deployed in a crescent line on either side of the contact team; a metallic clatter as weapons were checked. A shadow fell in front of them as a combat-car moved into position above.

"What do you suppose it means?" Meillard wondered.

"Terrans, go home." He drew a frown from Meillard with the suggestion. "Maybe it's supposed to intimidate us."

"They're probably doing it to encourage themselves," Anna de Jong, the psychologist, said. "I'll bet they're really scared stiff."

"I see how they're blowing it," Gofredo said. "The man who's walking behind it has a hand-bellows." He raised his voice. "Fix bayonets! These people don't know anything about rifles, but they know what spears are. They have some of their own."

So they had. The six who walked in the lead were unarmed, unless the thing one of them carried was a spear. So, it seemed, were the horn-bearers. Behind them, however, in an open-order skirmish-line, came fifty-odd with weapons. Most of them had spears, the points glinting redly. Bronze, with a high copper content. A few had bows. They came slowly; details became more plainly visible.

The leader wore a long yellow robe; the thing in his hand was a bronze-headed staff. Three of his companions also wore robes; the other two were bare-legged in short tunics. The horn-bearers wore either robes or tunics; the spearmen and bowmen behind either wore tunics or were naked except for breechclouts. All wore sandals. They were red-brown in color, completely hairless; they had long necks, almost chinless lower jaws, and fleshy, beaklike noses that gave them an avian appearance which was heightened by red crests, like roosters' combs, on the tops of their heads.

"Well, aren't they something to see?" Lillian Ransby, the linguist asked.

"I wonder how we look to them," Paul Meillard said.

That was something to wonder about, too. The differences between one and another of the Terrans must puzzle them. Paul Meillard, as close to being a pure Negro as anybody in the Seventh Century of the Atomic Era was to being pure anything. Lillian Ransby, almost ash-blond. Major Gofredo, barely over the minimum Service height requirement; his name was Old Terran Spanish, but his ancestry must have been Polynesian, Amerind and Mongolian. Karl Dorver, the sociographer, six feet six, with red hair. Bennet Fayon, the biologist and physiologist, plump, pink-faced and balding. Willi Schallenmacher, with a bushy black beard. . . .

They didn't have any ears, he noticed, and then he was taking stock of the things they wore and carried. Belts, with pouches, and knives with flat bronze blades and riveted handles. Three of the delegation had small flutes hung by cords around their necks, and a fourth had a reed Pan-pipe. No shields, and no swords; that was good. Swords and shields mean organized warfare, possibly a warrior-caste. This crowd weren't warriors. The spearmen and bowmen weren't arrayed for battle, but for a drive-hunt, with the bows behind the spears to stop anything that broke through the line.

"All right; let's go meet them." The querulous, uncertain note was gone from Meillard's voice; he knew what to do and how to do it.

Gofredo called to the Marines to stand fast. Then they were advancing to meet the natives, and when they were twenty feet apart, both groups halted. The horn stopped blowing. The one in the yellow robe lifted his staff and said something that sounded like, *"Tweedle-eedle-oodly-eenk."*

The horn, he saw, was made of strips of leather, wound spirally and coated with some kind of varnish. Everything these people had was carefully and finely made. An old culture, but a static one. Probably tradition-bound as all get-out.

Meillard was raising his hands; solemnly he addressed the natives:

"'Twas brillig and the slithy toves were whooping it up in the Malemute Saloon, and the kid that handled the music box did gyre and gimble in the wabe, and back of the bar in a solo game all mimsy were the borogoves, and the mome raths outgabe the lady that's known as Lou."

That was supposed to show them that we, too, have a spoken language, to prove that their language and ours were mutually incomprehensible, and to demonstrate the need for devising a means of communication. At least that was what the book said. It demonstrated nothing of the sort to this crowd. It scared them. The dignitary with the staff twittered excitedly. One of his companions agreed with him at length. Another started to reach for his knife, then remembered his manners. The bellowsman pumped a few blasts on the horn.

"What do you think of the language?" he asked Lillian.

"They all sound that bad, when you first hear them. Give them a few seconds, and then we'll have Phase Two."

When the gibbering and skreeking began to fall off, she stepped forward. Lillian was, herself, a good test of how human aliens were; this gang weren't human enough to whistle at her. She touched herself on the breast. "Me," she said.

The natives seemed shocked. She repeated the gesture and the word, then turned and addressed Paul Meillard. "You."

"Me," Meillard said, pointing to himself. Then he said, "You," to Luis Gofredo. It went around the contact team; when it came to him, he returned it to point of origin.

"I don't think they get it at all," he added in a whisper.

"They ought to," Lillian said. "Every language has a word for self and a word for person-addressed."

"Well, look at them," Karl Dorver invited. "Six different opinions about what we mean, and now the band's starting an argument of their own."

"Phase Two-A," Lillian said firmly, stepping forward. She pointed to herself. "Me — Lillian Ransby. Lillian Ransby — me *name*. You — *name?*"

"*Bwoooo!*" the spokesman screamed in horror, clutching his staff as though to shield it from profanation. The others howled like a hound-pack at a full moon, except one of the short-tunic boys, who was slapping himself on the head with both hands and yodeling. The horn-crew hastily swung their piece around at the Terrans, pumping frantically.

"What do you suppose I said?" Lillian asked.

"Oh, something like, 'Curse your gods, death to your king, and spit in your mother's face,' I suppose."

"Let me try it," Gofredo said.

The little Marine major went through the same routine. At his first word, the uproar stopped; before he was through, the natives' faces were sagging and crumbling into expressions of utter and heartbroken grief.

"It's not as bad as all that, is it?" he said. "You try it, Mark."

"Me . . . Mark . . . Howell. . . ." They looked bewildered.

"Let's try objects, and play-acting," Lillian suggested. "They're farmers; they ought to have a word for water."

*T*hey spent almost an hour at it. They poured out two gallons of water, pretended to be thirsty, gave each other drinks. The natives simply couldn't agree on the word, in their own language, for water. That or else they missed the point of the whole act. They tried fire, next. The efficiency of a steel hatchet was impressive, and so was the sudden flame of a pocket-lighter, but no word for fire emerged, either.

"Ah, to Nifflheim with it!" Luis Gofredo cried in exasperation. "We're getting nowhere at five times light speed. Give them their presents and send them home, Paul."

"Sheath-knives; they'll have to be shown how sharp they are," he suggested. "Red bandannas. And costume jewelry."

"How about something to eat, Bennet?" Meillard asked Fayon.

"Extee Three, and C-H trade candy," Fayon said. Field Ration, Extraterrestrial Service, Type Three, could be eaten by anything with a carbon-hydrogen metabolism, and so could the trade candy. "Nothing else, though, till we have some idea what goes on inside them."

Dorver thought the six members of the delegation would be persons of special consequence, and should have something extra. That was probably so. Dorver was as quick to pick up clues to an alien social order as he was, himself, to deduce a culture pattern from a few artifacts. He and Lillian went back to the landing craft to collect the presents.

Everybody, horn-detail, armed guard and all, got one ten-inch bowie knife and sheath, a red bandanna neckcloth, and a piece of flashy junk jewelry. The (town council? prominent citizens? or what?) also received a colored table-spread apiece; these were draped over their shoulders and fastened with two-inch plastic pins advertising the candidacy of somebody for President of the Federation Member Republic of Venus a couple of elections ago. They all looked woebegone about it; that would be their expression of joy. Different type nerves and different facial musculature, Fayon thought. As soon as they sampled the Extee Three and candy, they looked crushed under all the sorrows of the galaxy.

By pantomime and pointing to the sun, Meillard managed to inform them that the next day, when the sun was in the same position, the Terrans would visit their village, bringing more gifts. The natives were quite agreeable, but Meillard was disgruntled that he had to use sign-talk. The natives started off toward the village on the mound, munching Extee Three and trying out their new knives. This time tomorrow, half of them would have bandaged thumbs.

The Marine riflemen and submachine-gunners were coming in, slinging their weapons and lighting cigarettes. A couple of Navy technicians were getting a snooper — a thing shaped like a short-tailed tadpole, six feet long by three at the widest, fitted with visible-light and infra-red screen pickups and crammed with detection instruments — ready to relieve the combat car over the village. The contact team crowded into the Number One landing craft, which had been fitted out as a temporary headquarters. Prefab-hut elements were already being unloaded from the other craft.

Everybody felt that a drink was in order, even if it was two hours short of cocktail time. They carried bottles and glasses and ice to the front of the landing craft and sat down in front of the battery of view and communication screens. The central screen was a two-way, tuned to one in the officers' lounge aboard the *Hubert Penrose,* two hundred miles above. In it, also provided with drinks, were Captain Guy Vindinho and two other Navy officers, and a Marine captain in shipboard blues. Like Gofredo, Vindinho must have gotten into the Service on tiptoe; he had a bald dome and a red beard, and he always looked as though he were gloating because nobody knew that his name was really Rumplestiltskin. He had been watching the contact by screen. He lifted his glass toward Meillard.

"Over the hump, Paul?"

Meillard raised his drink to Vindinho. "Over the first one. There's a whole string of them ahead. At least, we sent them away happy. I hope."

"You're going to make permanent camp where you are now?" one of the other officers asked. Lieutenant-Commander Dave Questell; ground engineering and construction officer. "What do you need?"

There were two viewscreens from pickups aboard the 2500-foot battle cruiser. One, at ten-power magnification, gave a maplike view of the broad valley and the uplands and mountain foothills to the south. It was only by tracing the course of the main river and its tributaries that they could find the tiny spot of the native village, and they couldn't see the landing craft at all. The other, at a hundred power, showed the oblong mound, with the village on its flat top, little dots around a circular central plaza. They could see the two turtle-shaped landing-craft, and the combat car, that had been circling over the mound, landing beside them, and, sometimes, a glint of sunlight from the snooper that had taken its place.

The snooper was also transmitting in, to another screen, from two hundred feet above the village. From the sound outlet came an incessant gibber of native voices. There were over a hundred houses, all small and square, with pyramidal roofs. On the end of the mound toward the Terran camp, animals of at least four different species were crowded, cattle that had been herded up from the meadows at the first alarm. The open circle in the middle of the village was crowded, and more natives lined the low palisade along the edge of the mound.

"Well, we're going to stay here till we learn the language," Meillard was saying. "This is the best place for it. It's completely isolated, forests on both sides, and seventy miles to the nearest other village. If we're careful, we can stay here as long as we want to and nobody'll find out about us. Then, after we can talk with these people, we'll go to the big town."

*T*he big town was two hundred and fifty miles down the valley, at the forks of the main river, a veritable metropolis of almost three thousand people. That was where the treaty would have to be negotiated.

"You'll want more huts. You'll want a water tank, and a pipeline to that stream below you, and a pump," Questell said. "You think a month?"

Meillard looked at Lillian Ransby. "What do you think?"

"Poodly-doodly-oodly-foodle," she said. "You saw how far we didn't get this afternoon. All we found out was that none of the standard procedures work at all." She made a tossing gesture over her shoulder. "There goes the book; we have to do it off the cuff from here."

"Suppose we make another landing, back in the mountains, say two or three hundred miles south of you," Vindinho said. "It's not right to keep the rest aboard two hundred miles off planet, and you won't be wanting liberty parties coming down where you are."

"The country over there looks uninhabited," Meillard said. "No villages, anyhow. That wouldn't hurt, at all."

"Well, it'll suit me," Charley Loughran, the xeno-naturalist, said. "I want a chance to study the life-forms in a state of nature."

Vindinho nodded. "Luis, do you anticipate any trouble with this crowd here?" he asked.

"How about it, Mark? What do they look like to you? Warlike?"

"No." He stated the opinion he had formed. "I had a close look at their weapons when they came in for their presents. Hunting arms. Most of the spears have cross-guards, usually wooden, lashed on, to prevent a wounded animal from running up the spear-shaft at the hunter. They made boar-spears like that on Terra a thousand years ago. Maybe they have to fight raiding parties from the hills once in a while, but not often enough for them to develop special fighting weapons or techniques."

"Their village is fortified," Meillard mentioned.

"I question that," Gofredo differed. "There won't be more than a total of five hundred there; call that a fighting strength of two hundred, to defend a twenty-five-?hundred-?meter perimeter, with woodchoppers' axes and bows and spears. If you notice, there's no wall around the village itself. That palisade is just a fence."

"Why would they mound the village up?" Questell, in the screen wondered. "You don't think the river gets up that high, do you? Because if it does —"

Schallenmacher shook his head. "There just isn't enough water-shed, and there's too much valley. I'll be very much surprised if that stream, there" — he nodded at the hundred-power screen — "ever gets more than six inches over the bank."

"I don't know what those houses are built of. This is all alluvial country; building stone would be almost unobtainable. I don't see anything like a brick kiln. I don't see any evidence of irrigation, either, so there must be plenty of rainfall. If they use adobe, or sun-dried brick, houses would start to crumble in a few years, and they would be pulled down and the rubble shoved aside to make room for a new house. The village has been rising on its own ruins, probably shifting back and forth from one end of that mound to the other."

"If that's it, they've been there a long time," Karl Dorver said. "And how far have they advanced?"

"Early bronze; I'll bet they still use a lot of stone implements. Pre-dynastic Egypt, or very early Tigris-Euphrates, in Terran terms. I can't see any evidence that they have the wheel. They have draft animals; when we were coming down, I saw a few of them pulling pole travoises. I'd say they've been farming for a long time. They have quite a diversity of crops, and I suspect that they have some idea of crop-rotation. I'm amazed at their musical instruments; they seem to have put more skill into making them than anything

else. I'm going to take a jeep, while they're all in the village, and
have a look around the fields, now."

Charley Loughran went along for specimens, and, for the ride,
Lillian Ransby. Most of his guesses, he found, had been correct.
He found a number of pole travoises, from which the animals had
been unhitched in the first panic when the landing craft had been
coming down. Some of them had big baskets permanently at-
tached. There were drag-marks everywhere in the soft ground, but
not a single wheel track. He found one plow, cunningly put
together with wooden pegs and rawhide lashings; the point was
stone, and it would only score a narrow groove, not a proper
furrow. It was, however, fitted with a big bronze ring to which a
draft animal could be hitched. Most of the cultivation seemed to
have been done with spades and hoes. He found a couple of each,
bronze, cast flat in an open-top mold. They hadn't learned to make
composite molds.

There was an even wider variety of crops than he had expected:
two cereals, a number of different root-plants, and a lot of different
legumes, and things like tomatoes and pumpkins.

"Bet these people had a pretty good life, here — before the
Terrans came," Charley observed.

"Don't say that in front of Paul," Lillian warned. "He has
enough to worry about now, without starting him on whether we'll
do these people more harm than good."

Two more landing craft had come down from the *Hubert Penrose*;
they found Dave Questell superintending the unloading of more
prefab-huts, and two were already up that had been brought down
with the first landing.

A name for the planet had also arrived.

"Svantovit," Karl Dorver told him. "Principal god of the Baltic
Slavs, about three thousand years ago. Guy Vindinho dug it out
of the 'Encyclopedia of Mythology.' Svantovit was represented as
holding a bow in one hand and a horn in the other."

"Well, that fits. What will we call the natives; Svantovitians, or
Svantovese?"

"Well, Paul wanted to call them Svantovese, but Luis persuaded
him to call them Svants. He said everybody'd call them that,
anyhow, so we might as well make it official from the start."

"We can call the language Svantovese," Lillian decided. "After
dinner, I am going to start playing back recordings and running
off audiovisuals. I will be so happy to know that I have a name
for what I'm studying. Probably be all I will know."

*A*fter dinner, he and Karl and Paul went into a huddle on what sort of gifts to give the natives, and the advisability of trading with them, and for what. Nothing too far in advance of their present culture level. Wheels; they could be made in the fabricating shop aboard the ship.

"You know, it's odd," Karl Dorver said. "These people here have never seen a wheel, and, except in documentary or historical-drama films, neither have a lot of Terrans."

That was true. As a means of transportation, the wheel had been completely obsolete since the development of contragravity, six centuries ago. Well, a lot of Terrans in the Year Zero had never seen a suit of armor, or an harquebus, or even a tinderbox or a spinning wheel.

Wheelbarrows; now there was something they'd find useful. He screened Max Milzer, in charge of the fabricating and repair shops on the ship. Max had never even heard of a wheelbarrow.

"I can make them up, Mark; better send me some drawings, though. Did you just invent it?"

"As far as I know, a man named Leonardo da Vinci invented it, in the Sixth Century Pre-Atomic. How soon can you get me half a dozen of them?"

"Well, let's see. Welded sheet metal, and pipe for the frame and handles. I'll have some of them for you by noon tomorrow. Now, about hoes; how tall are these people, and how long are their arms, and how far can they stoop over?"

*T*hey were all up late, that night. So were the Svants; there was a fire burning in the middle of the village, and watch-fires along the edge of the mound. Luis Gofredo was just as distrustful of them as they were of the Terrans; he kept the camp lighted, a strong guard on the alert, and the area of darkness beyond infra red lighted and covered by photoelectric sentries on the ground and snoopers in the air. Like Paul Meillard, Luis Gofredo was a worrier and a pessimist. Everything happened for the worst in this worst of all possible galaxies, and if anything could conceivably go wrong, it infallibly would. That was probably why he was still alive and had never had a command massacred.

The wheelbarrows, four of them, came down from the ship by midmorning. With them came a grindstone, a couple of crosscut saws, and a lot of picks and shovels and axes, and cases of sheath knives and mess gear and miscellaneous trade goods, including a lot of the empty wine and whisky bottles that had been hoarded for the past four years.

At lunch, the talk was almost exclusively about the language problem. Lillian Ransby, who had not gotten to sleep before sunrise and had just gotten up, was discouraged.

"I don't know what we're going to do next," she admitted. "Glenn Orent and Anna and I were on it all night, and we're nowhere. We have about a hundred wordlike sounds isolated, and twenty or so are used repeatedly, and we can't assign a meaning to any of them. And none of the Svants ever reacted the same way twice to anything we said to them. There's just no one-to-one relationship anywhere."

"I'm beginning to doubt they have a language," the Navy intelligence officer said. "Sure, they make a lot of vocal noise. So do chipmunks."

"They have to have a language," Anna de Jong declared. "No sapient thought is possible without verbalization."

"Well, no society like that is possible without some means of communication," Karl Dorver supported her from the other flank. He seemed to have made that point before. "You know," he added, "I'm beginning to wonder if it mightn't be telepathy."

He evidently hadn't suggested that before. The others looked at him in surprise. Anna started to say, "Oh, I doubt if —" and then stopped.

"I know, the race of telepaths is an old gimmick that's been used in new-planet adventure stories for centuries, but maybe we've finally found one."

"I don't like it, Karl," Loughran said. "If they're telepaths, why don't they understand us? And if they're telepaths, why do they talk at all? And you can't convince me that this boodly-oodly-doodle of theirs isn't talking."

"Well, our neural structure and theirs won't be nearly alike," Fayon said. "I know, this analogy between telepathy and radio is full of holes, but it's good enough for this. Our wave length can't be picked up with their sets."

"The deuce it can't," Gofredo contradicted. "I've been bothered about that from the beginning. These people act as though they got meaning from us. Not the meaning we intend, but some meaning. When Paul made the gobbledygook speech, they all reacted in the same way — frightened, and then defensive. The you-me routine simply bewildered them, as we'd be at a set of semantically lucid but self-contradictory statements. When Lillian tried to introduce herself, they were shocked and horrified. . . ."

"It looked to me like actual physical disgust," Anna interpolated.

"When I tried it, they acted like a lot of puppies being petted, and when Mark tried it, they were simply baffled. I watched Mark explaining that steel knives were dangerously sharp; they got the demonstration, but when he tried to tie words onto it, it threw them completely."

"ALL RIGHT. Pass that," Loughran conceded. "But if they have telepathy, why do they use spoken words?"

"Oh, I can answer that," Anna said. "Say they communicated by speech originally, and developed their telepathic faculty slowly and without realizing it. They'd go on using speech, and since the message would be received telepathically ahead of the spoken message, nobody would pay any attention to the words as such. Everybody would have a spoken language of his own; it would be sort of the instrumental accompaniment to the song."

"Some of them don't bother speaking," Karl nodded. "They just toot."

"I'll buy that, right away," Loughran agreed. "In mating, or in group-danger situations, telepathy would be a race-survival characteristic. It would be selected for genetically, and the non-gifted strains would tend to die out."

It wouldn't do. It wouldn't do at all. He said so.

"Look at their technology. We either have a young race, just emerged from savagery, or an old, stagnant race. All indications seem to favor the latter. A young race would not have time to develop telepathy as Anna suggests. An old race would have gone much farther than these people have. Progress is a matter of communication and pooling ideas and discoveries. Make a trend-graph of technological progress on Terra; every big jump comes after an improvement in communications. The printing press; railways and steamships; the telegraph; radio. Then think how telepathy would speed up progress."

*T*he sun was barely past noon meridian before the Svants, who had ventured down into the fields at sunrise, were returning to the mound-village. In the snooper-screen, they could be seen coming up in tunics and breechclouts, entering houses, and emerging in long robes. There seemed to be no bows or spears in evidence, but the big horn sounded occasionally. Paul Meillard was pleased. Even if it had been by sign-talk, which he rated with worm-fishing for trout or shooting sitting rabbits, he had gotten something across to them.

When they went to the village, at 1500, they had trouble getting their lorry down. A couple of Marines in a jeep had to go in first to get the crowd out of the way. Several of the locals, including the one with the staff, joined with them; this quick cooperation delighted Meillard. When they had the lorry down and were all out of it, the dignitary with the staff, his scarlet tablecloth over his yellow robe, began an oration, apparently with every confidence that he was being understood. In spite of his objections at lunch, the telepathy theory was beginning to seem more persuasive.

"Give them the Shooting of Dan McJabberwock again," he told Meillard. "This is where we came in yesterday."

Something Meillard had noticed was exciting him. "Wait a moment. They're going to do something."

They were indeed. The one with the staff and three of his henchmen advanced. The staff bearer touched himself on the brow. *"Fwoonk,"* he said. Then he pointed to Meillard. *"Hoonkle,"* he said.

"They got it!" Lillian was hugging herself joyfully. "I knew they ought to!"

Meillard indicated himself and said, *"Fwoonk."*

That wasn't right. The village elder immediately corrected him. The word, it seemed, was, *"Fwoonk."*

His three companions agreed that that was the word for self, but that was as far as the agreement went. They rendered it, respectively, as *"Pwink," "Tweelt"* and *"Kroosh."*

Gofredo gave a barking laugh. He was right; anything that could go wrong would go wrong. Lillian used a word; it was not a ladylike word at all. The Svants looked at them as though wondering what could possibly be the matter. Then they went into a huddle, arguing vehemently. The argument spread, like a ripple in a pool; soon everybody was twittering vocally or blowing on flutes and Panpipes. Then the big horn started blaring. Immediately, Gofredo snatched the hand-phone of his belt radio and began speaking urgently into it.

"What are you doing, Luis?" Meillard asked anxiously.

"Calling the reserve in. I'm not taking chances on this." He spoke again into the phone, then called over his shoulder: "Rienet; three one-second bursts, in the air!"

A Marine pointed a submachine gun skyward and ripped off a string of shots, then another, and another. There was silence after the first burst. Then a frightful howling arose.

"Luis, you imbecile!" Meillard was shouting.

Gofredo jumped onto the top of an airjeep, where they could all see him; drawing his pistol, he fired twice into the air.

"Be quiet, all of you!" he shouted, as though that would do any good.

It did. Silence fell, bounced noisily, and then settled over the crowd. Gofredo went on talking to them: "Take it easy, now; easy." He might have been speaking to a frightened dog or a fractious horse. "Nobody's going to hurt you. This is nothing but the great noise-magic of the Terrans. . . ."

"Get the presents unloaded," Meillard was saying. "Make a big show of it. The table first."

The horn, which had started, stopped blowing. As they were getting off the long table and piling it with trade goods, another lorry came in, disgorging twenty Marine riflemen. They had their bayonets fixed; the natives looked apprehensively at the bare steel, but went on listening to Gofredo. Meillard pulled the (Lord Mayor? Archbishop? Lord of the Manor?) aside, and began making sign-talk to him.

When quiet was restored, Howell put a pick and shovel into a wheelbarrow and pushed them out into the space that had been cleared in front of the table. He swung the pick for a while, then shoveled the barrow full of ground. After pushing it around for a while, he dumped it back in the hole and leveled it off. Two Marines brought out an eight-inch log and chopped a couple of billets off it with an ax, then cut off another with one of the saws, split them up, and filled the wheelbarrow with the firewood.

The knives, jewelry and other small items would be no problem; they had enough of them to go around. The other stuff would be harder to distribute, and Paul Meillard and Karl Dorver were arguing about how to handle it. If they weren't careful, a lot of new bowie knives would get bloodied.

"Have them form a queue," Anna suggested. "That will give them the idea of equal sharing, and we'll be able to learn something about their status levels and social hierarchy and agonistic relations."

*T*he one with the staff took it as a matter of course that he
would go first; his associates began falling in behind him, and the
rest of the villagers behind them. Whether they'd gotten one the
day before or not, everybody was given a knife and a bandanna
and one piece of flashy junk-jewelry, also a stainless steel cup and
mess plate, a bucket, and an empty bottle with a cork. The women
didn't carry sheath knives, so they got Boy Scout knives on lan-
yards. They were all lavishly supplied with Extee Three and candy.
Any of the children who looked big enough to be trusted with
them got knives too, and plenty of candy.

Anna and Karl were standing where the queue was forming,
watching how they fell into line; so was Lillian, with an audiovisual
camera. Having seen that the Marine enlisted men were getting
the presents handed out properly, Howell strolled over to them.
Just as he came up, a couple approached hesitantly, a man in a
breechclout under a leather apron, and a woman, much smaller,
in a ragged and soiled tunic. As soon as they fell into line, another
Svant, in a blue robe, pushed them aside and took their place.

"Here, you can't do that!" Lillian cried. "Karl, make him step
back."

Karl was saying something about social status and precedence.
The couple tried to get into line behind the man who had pushed
them aside. Another villager tried to shove them out of his way.
Howell advanced, his right fist closing. Then he remembered that
he didn't know what he'd be punching; he might break the fellow's
neck, or his own knuckles. He grabbed the blue-robed Svant by
the wrist with both hands, kicked a foot out from under him, and
jerked, sending him flying for six feet and then sliding in the dust
for another couple of yards. He pushed the others back, and put
the couple into place in the line.

"Mark, you shouldn't have done that," Dorver was expostulat-
ing. "We don't know. . . ."

The Svant sat up, shaking his head groggily. Then he realized
what had been done to him. With a snarl of rage, he was on his
feet, his knife in his hand. It was a Terran bowie knife. Without
conscious volition, Howell's pistol was out and he was thumbing
the safety off.

The Svant stopped short, then dropped the knife, ducked his
head, and threw his arms over it to shield his comb. He backed
away a few steps, then turned and bolted into the nearest house.
The others, including the woman in the ragged tunic, were twit-

tering in alarm. Only the man in the leather apron was calm; he was saying, tonelessly, *"Ghrooogh-ghrooogh."*

Luis Gofredo was coming up on the double, followed by three of his riflemen.

"What happened, Mark? Trouble?"

"All over now." He told Gofredo what had happened. Dorver was still objecting:

". . . Social precedence; the Svant may have been right, according to local customs."

"Local customs be damned!" Gofredo became angry. "This is a Terran Federation handout; we make the rules, and one of them is, no pushing people out of line. Teach the buggers that now and we won't have to work so hard at it later." He called back over his shoulder, "Situation under control; get the show going again."

The natives were all grimacing heartbrokenly with pleasure. Maybe the one who got thrown on his ear — no, he didn't have any — was not one of the more popular characters in the village.

"You just pulled your gun, and he dropped the knife and ran?" Gofredo asked. "And the others were scared, too?"

"That's right. They all saw you fire yours; the noise scared them."

Gofredo nodded. "We'll avoid promiscuous shooting, then. No use letting them find out the noise won't hurt them any sooner than we have to."

Paul Meillard had worked out a way to distribute the picks and shovels and axes. Considering each house as representing a family unit, which might or might not be the case, there were picks and shovels enough to go around, and an ax for every third house. They took them around in an airjeep and left them at the doors. The houses, he found, weren't adobe at all. They were built of logs, plastered with adobe on the outside. That demolished his theory that the houses were torn down periodically, and left the mound itself unexplained.

The wheelbarrows and the grindstone and the two crosscut saws were another matter. Nobody was quite sure that the (nobility? capitalist-class? politicians? prominent citizens?) wouldn't simply appropriate them for themselves. Paul Meillard was worried about that; everybody else was willing to let matters take their course. Before they were off the ground in their vehicles, a violent dispute had begun, with a bedlam of jabbering and shrieking. By the time they were landing at the camp, the big laminated leather horn had begun to bellow.

*O*ne of the huts had been fitted as contact-team headquarters, with all the view and communication screens installed, and one end partitioned off and soundproofed for Lillian to study recordings in. It was cocktail time when they returned; conversationally, it was a continuation from lunch. Karl Dorver was even more convinced than ever of his telepathic hypothesis, and he had completely converted Anna de Jong to it.

"Look at that." He pointed at the snooper screen, which gave a view of the plaza from directly above. "They're reaching an agreement already."

So they seemed to be, though upon what was less apparent. The horn had stopped, and the noise was diminishing. The odd thing was that peace was being restored, or was restoring itself, as the uproar had begun — outwardly from the center of the plaza to the periphery of the crowd. The same thing had happened when Gofredo had ordered the submachine gun fired, and, now that he recalled, when he had dealt with the line-crasher.

"Suppose a few of them, in the middle, are agreed," Anna said. "They are all thinking in unison, combining their telepathic powers. They dominate those nearest to them, who join and amplify their telepathic signal, and it spreads out through the whole group. A mental chain-reaction."

"That would explain the mechanism of community leadership, and I'd been wondering about that," Dorver said, becoming more excited. "It's a mental aristocracy; an especially gifted group of telepaths, in agreement and using their powers in concert, implanting their opinions in the minds of all the others. I'll bet the purpose of the horn is to distract the thoughts of the others, so that they can be more easily dominated. And the noise of the shots shocked them out of communication with each other; no wonder they were frightened."

Bennet Fayon was far from convinced. "So far, this telepathy theory is only an assumption. I find it a lot easier to assume some fundamental difference between the way they translate sound into sense-data and the way we do. We *think* those combs on top of their heads are their external hearing organs, but we have no idea what's back of them, or what kind of a neural hookup is connected to them. I wish I knew how these people dispose of their dead. I need a couple of fresh cadavers. Too bad they aren't warlike. Nothing like a good bloody battle to advance the science of anatomy, and what we don't know about Svant anatomy is practically the entire subject."

"I should imagine the animals hear in the same way," Meillard said. "When the wagon wheels and the hoes and the blacksmith tools come down from the ship, we'll trade for cattle."

"When they make the second landing in the mountains, I'm going to do a lot of hunting," Loughran added. "I'll get wild animals for you."

"Well, I'm going to assume that the vocal noises they make are meaningful speech," Lillian Ransby said. "So far, I've just been trying to analyze them for phonetic values. Now I'm going to analyze them for sound-wave patterns. No matter what goes on inside their private nervous systems, the sounds exist as waves in the public atmosphere. I'm going to assume that the Lord Mayor and his stooges were all trying to say the same thing when they were pointing to themselves, and I'm going to see if all four of those sounds have any common characteristic."

By the time dinner was over, they were all talking in circles, none of them hopefully. They all made recordings of the speech about the slithy toves in the Malemute Saloon; Lillian wanted to find out what was different about them. Luis Gofredo saw to it that the camp itself would be visible-lighted, and beyond the lights he set up more photoelectric robot sentries and put a couple of snoopers to circling on contragravity, with infra-red lights and receptors. He also insisted that all his own men and all Dave Questell's Navy construction engineers keep their weapons ready to hand. The natives in the village were equally distrustful. They didn't herd the cattle up from the meadows where they had been pastured, but they lighted watch-fires along the edge of the mound as soon as it became dark.

*I*t was three hours after nightfall when something on the indicator-board for the robot sentries went off like a startled rattlesnake. Everybody, talking idly or concentrating on writing up the day's observations, stiffened. Luis Gofredo, dozing in a chair, was on his feet instantly and crossing the hut to the instruments. His second-in-command, who had been playing chess with Willi Schallenmacher, rose and snatched his belt from the back of his chair, putting it on.

"Take it easy," Gofredo said. "Probably just a cow or a horse — local equivalent — that's strayed over from the other side."

He sat down in front of one of the snooper screens and twisted knobs on the remote controls. The monochrome view, transformed from infra red, rotated as the snooper circled and changed course. The other screen showed the camp receding and the area around it widening as its snooper gained altitude.

"It's not a big party," Gofredo was saying. "I can't see — Oh, yes I can. Only two of them."

The humanoid figures, one larger than the other, were moving cautiously across the fields, crouching low. The snooper went down toward them, and then he recognized them. The man and woman whom the blue-robed villager had tried to shove out of the queue, that afternoon. Gofredo recognized them, too.

"Your friends, Mark. Harry," he told his subordinate, "go out and pass the word around. Only two, and we think they're friendly. Keep everybody out of sight; we don't want to scare them away."

The snooper followed closely behind them. The man was no longer wearing his apron; the woman's tunic was even more tattered and soiled. She was leading him by the hand. Now and then, she would stop and turn her head to the rear. The snooper over the mound showed nothing but half a dozen fire-watchers dozing by their fires. Then the pair were at the edge of the camp lights. As they advanced, they seemed to realize that they had passed a point-of-no-return. They straightened and came forward steadily, the woman seeming to be guiding her companion.

"What's happening, Mark?"

It was Lillian; she must have just come out of the soundproof speech-lab.

"You know them; the pair in the queue, this afternoon. I think we've annexed a couple of friendly natives."

They all went outside. The two natives, having come into the camp, had stopped. For a moment, the man in the breechclout seemed undecided whether he was more afraid to turn and run than advance. The woman, holding his hand, led him forward. They were both bruised, and both had minor cuts, and neither of them had any of the things that had been given to them that afternoon.

"Rest of the gang beat them up and robbed them," Gofredo began angrily.

"See what you did?" Dorver began. "According to their own customs, they had no right to be ahead of those others, and now you've gotten them punished for it."

"I'd have done more to that fellow then Mark did, if I'd been there when it happened." The Marine officer turned to Meillard. "Look, this is your show, Paul; how you run it is your job. But in your place, I'd take that pair back to the village and have them point out who beat them up, and teach the whole gang of them a lesson. If you're going to colonize this planet, you're going to have to establish Federation law, and Federation law says you mustn't gang up on people and beat and rob them. We don't have to speak Svantese to make them understand what we'll put up with and what we won't."

"Later, Luis. After we've gotten a treaty with somebody." Meillard broke off. "Watch this!"

The woman was making sign-talk. She pointed to the village on the mound. Then, with her hands, she shaped a bucket like the ones that had been given to them, and made a snatching gesture away from herself. She indicated the neckcloths, and the sheath knife and the other things, and snatched them away too. She made beating motions, and touched her bruises and the man's. All the time, she was talking excitedly, in a high, shrill voice. The man made the same *ghroogh-ghroogh* noises that he had that afternoon.

"No; we can't take any punitive action. Not now," Meillard said. "But we'll have to do something for them."

Vengeance, it seemed, wasn't what they wanted. The woman made vehement gestures of rejection toward the village, then bowed, placing her hands on her brow. The man imitated her obeisance, then they both straightened. The woman pointed to herself and to the man, and around the circle of huts and landing craft. She began scuttling about, picking up imaginary litter and sweeping with an imaginary broom. The man started pounding with an imaginary hammer, then chopping with an imaginary ax.

Lillian was clapping her hands softly. "Good; got it the first time. 'You let us stay; we work for you.' How about it, Paul?"

Meillard nodded. "Punitive action's unadvisable, but we will show our attitude by taking them in. You tell them, Luis; these people seem to like your voice."

Gofredo put a hand on each of their shoulders. "You . . . stay . . . with us." He pointed around the camp. "You . . . stay . . . this . . . place."

Their faces broke into that funny just-before-tears expression that meant happiness with them. The man confined his vocal expressions to his odd *ghroogh-ghroogh*-ing; the woman twittered joyfully. Gofredo put a hand on the woman's shoulder, pointed to the man and from him back to her. "Unh?" he inquired.

The woman put a hand on the man's head, then brought it down to within a foot of the ground. She picked up the imaginary infant and rocked it in her arms, then set it down and grew it up until she had her hand on the top of the man's head again.

"That was good, Mom," Gofredo told her. "Now, you and Sonny come along; we'll issue you equipment and find you billets." He added, "What in blazes are we going to feed them; Extee Three?"

*T*hey gave them replacements for all the things that had been taken away from them. They gave the man a one-piece suit of Marine combat coveralls; Lillian gave the woman a lavender bathrobe, and Anna contributed a red scarf. They found them quarters in one end of a store shed, after making sure that there was nothing they could get at that would hurt them or that they could damage. They gave each of them a pair of blankets and a pneumatic mattress, which delighted them, although the cots puzzled them at first.

"What do you think about feeding them, Bennet?" Meillard asked, when the two Svants had gone to bed and they were back in the headquarters hut. "You said the food on this planet is safe for Terrans."

"So I did, and it is, but the rule's not reversible. Things we eat might kill them," Fayon said. "Meats will be especially dangerous. And no caffein, and no alcohol."

"Alcohol won't hurt them," Schallenmacher said. "I saw big jars full of fermenting fruit-mash back of some of those houses; in about a year, it ought to be fairly good wine. C_2H_5OH is the same on any planet."

"Well, we'll get native foodstuffs tomorrow," Meillard said. "We'll have to do that by signs, too," he regretted.

"Get Mom to help you; she's pretty sharp," Lillian advised. "But I think Sonny's the village half-wit."

Anna de Jong agreed. "Even if we don't understand Svant psychology, that's evident; he's definitely subnormal. The way he clings to his mother for guidance is absolutely pathetic. He's a mature adult, but mentally he's still a little child."

"That may explain it!" Dorver cried. "A mental defective, in a community of telepaths, constantly invading the minds of others with irrational and disgusting thoughts; no wonder he is rejected and persecuted. And in a community on this culture level, the mother of an abnormal child is often regarded with superstitious detestation —"

"Yes, of course!" Anna de Jong instantly agreed, and began to go into the villagers' hostility to both mother and son; both of them were now taking the telepathy hypothesis for granted.

Well, maybe so. He turned to Lillian.

"What did you find out?"

"Well, there is a common characteristic in all four sounds. A little patch on the screen at seventeen-twenty cycles. The odd thing is that when I try to repeat the sound, it isn't there."

Odd indeed. If a Svant said something, he made sound waves; if she imitated the sound, she ought to imitate the wave pattern. He said so, and she agreed.

"But come back here and look at this," she invited.

She had been using a visibilizing analyzer; in it, a sound was broken by a set of filters into frequency-groups, translated into light from dull red to violet paling into pure white. It photographed the light-pattern on high-speed film, automatically developed it, and then made a print-copy and projected the film in slow motion on a screen. When she pressed a button, a recorded voice said, *"Fwoonk."* An instant later, a pattern of vertical lines in various colors and lengths was projected on the screen.

"Those green lines," she said. "That's it. Now, watch this."

She pressed another button, got the photoprint out of a slot, and propped it beside the screen. Then she picked up a hand-phone and said, *"Fwoonk,"* into it. It sounded like the first one, but the pattern that danced onto the screen was quite different. Where the green had been, there was a patch of pale-blue lines. She ran the other three Svants' voices, each saying, presumably, "Me." Some were mainly up in blue, others had a good deal of yellow and orange, but they all had the little patch of green lines.

"Well, that seems to be the information," he said. "The rest is just noise."

"Maybe one of them is saying, 'John Doe, *me*, son of Joe Blow,' and another is saying, 'Tough guy, *me*; lick anybody in town.'"

"All in one syllable?" Then he shrugged. How did he know what these people could pack into one syllable? He picked up the hand-phone and said, "Fwoonk," into it. The pattern, a little deeper in color and with longer lines, was recognizably like hers, and unlike any of the Svants'.

*T*he others came in, singly and in pairs and threes. They watched the colors dance on the screen to picture the four Svant words which might or might not all mean *me*. They tried to duplicate them. Luis Gofredo and Willi Schallenmacher came closest of anybody. Bennet Fayon was still insisting that the Svants had a perfectly comprehensible language — to other Svants. Anna de Jong had started to veer a little away from the Dorver Hypothesis. There was a difference between event-level sound, which was a series of waves of alternately crowded and rarefied molecules of air, and object-level sound, which was an auditory sensation inside the nervous system, she admitted. That, Fayon crowed, was what he'd been saying all along; their auditory system was probably such that *fwoonk* and *pwink* and *tweelt* and *kroosh* all sounded alike to them.

By this time, *fwoonk* and *pwink* and *tweelt* and *kroosh* had become swear words among the joint Space Navy-Colonial Office contact team.

"Well, if I hear the two sounds alike, why doesn't the analyzer hear them alike?" Karl Dorver demanded.

"It has better ears than you do, Karl. Look how many different frequencies there are in that word, all crowding up behind each other," Lillian said. "But it isn't sensitive or selective enough. I'm going to see what Ayesha Keithley can do about building me a better one."

Ayesha was signals and detection officer on the *Hubert Penrose*. Dave Questell mentioned that she'd had a hard day, and was probably making sack-time, and she wouldn't welcome being called at 0130. Nobody seemed to have realized that it had gotten that late.

"Well, I'll call the ship and have a recording made for her for when she gets up. But till we get something that'll sort this mess out and make sense of it, I'm stopped."

"You're stopped, period, Lillian," Dorver told her. "What these people gibber at us doesn't even make as much sense as the Shooting of Dan McJabberwock. The real information is conveyed by telepathy."

*L*ieutenant j.g. Ayesha Keithley was on the screen the next morning while they were eating breakfast. She was a blonde, like Lillian.

"I got your message; you seem to have problems, don't you?"

"Speaking conservatively, yes. You see what we're up against?"

"You don't know what their vocal organs are like, do you?" the girl in naval uniform in the screen asked.

Lillian shook her head. "Bennet Fayon's hoping for a war, or an epidemic, or something to break out, so that he can get a few cadavers to dissect."

"Well, he'll find that they're pretty complex," Ayesha Keithley said. "I identified stick-and-slip sounds and percussion sounds, and plucked-string sounds, along with the ordinary hiss-and-buzz speech-sounds. Making a vocoder to reproduce that speech is going to be fun. Just what are you using, in the way of equipment?"

Lillian was still talking about that when the two landing craft from the ship were sighted, coming down. Charley Loughran and Willi Schallenmacher, who were returning to the *Hubert Penrose* to join the other landing party, began assembling their luggage. The others went outside, Howell among them.

Mom and Sonny were watching the two craft grow larger and closer above, keeping close to a group of spacemen; Sonny was looking around excitedly, while Mom clung to his arm, like a hen with an oversized chick. The reasoning was clear — these people knew all about big things that came down out of the sky and weren't afraid of them; stick close to them, and it would be perfectly safe. Sonny saw the contact team emerging from their hut and grabbed his mother's arm, pointing. They both beamed happily; that expression didn't look sad, at all, now that you knew what it meant. Sonny began ghroogh-ghrooghing hideously; Mom hushed him with a hand over his mouth, and they both made eating gestures, rubbed their abdomens comfortably, and pointed toward the mess hut. Bennet Fayon was frightened. He turned and started on the double toward the cook, who was standing in the doorway of the hut, calling out to him.

The cook spoke inaudibly. Fayon stopped short. "Unholy Saint Beelzebub, no!" he cried. The cook said something in reply, shrugging. Fayon came back, talking to himself.

"Terran carniculture pork," he said, when he returned. "Zarathustra pool-ball fruit. Potato-flour hotcakes, with Baldur honey and Odin flameberry jam. And two big cups of coffee apiece. It's a miracle they aren't dead now. If they're alive for lunch, we won't need to worry about feeding them anything we eat, but I'm glad somebody else has the moral responsibility for this."

Lillian Ransby came out of the headquarters hut. "Ayesha's coming down this afternoon, with a lot of equipment," she said. "We're not exactly going to count air molecules in the sound waves, but we'll do everything short of that. We'll need more lab space, soundproofed."

"Tell Dave Questell what you want," Meillard said. "Do you really think you can get anything?"

She shrugged. "If there's anything there to get. How long it'll take is another question."

*T*he two sixty-foot collapsium-armored turtles settled to the ground and went off contragravity. The ports opened, and things began being floated off on lifter-skids: framework for the water tower, and curved titanium sheets for the tank. Anna de Jong said something about hot showers, and not having to take anymore sponge-baths. Howell was watching the stuff come off the other landing craft. A dozen pairs of four-foot wagon wheels, with axles. Hoes, in bundles. Scythe blades. A hand forge, with a crank-driven fan blower, and a hundred and fifty pound anvil, and sledges and cutters and swages and tongs.

Everybody was busy, and Mom and Sonny were fidgeting, gesturing toward the work with their own empty hands. *Hey, boss; whatta we gonna do?* He patted them on the shoulders.

"Take it easy." He hoped his tone would convey nonurgency. "We'll find something for you to do."

He wasn't particularly happy about most of what was coming off. Giving these Svants tools was fine, but it was more important to give them technologies. The people on the ship hadn't thought of that. These wheels, now; machined steel hubs, steel rims, tubular steel spokes, drop-forged and machined axles. The Svants wouldn't be able to copy them in a thousand years. Well, in a hundred, if somebody showed them where and how to mine iron and how to smelt and work it. And how to build a steam engine.

He went over and pulled a hoe out of one of the bundles. Blades stamped out with a power press, welded to tubular steel handles. Well, wood for hoe handles was hard to come by on a spaceship, even a battle cruiser almost half a mile in diameter; he had to admit that. And they were about two thousand percent more efficient than the bronze scrapers the Svants used. That wasn't the idea, though. Even supposing that the first wave of colonists came out in a year and a half, it would be close to twenty years before Terran-operated factories would be in mass production for the native trade. The idea was to teach these people to make better things for themselves; give them a leg up, so that the next generation would be ready for contragravity and nuclear and electric power.

Mom didn't know what to make of any of it. Sonny did, though; he was excited, grabbing Howell's arm, pointing, saying, *"Ghroogh! Ghroogh!"* He pointed at the wheels, and then made a stooping, lifting and pushing gesture. *Like wheelbarrow?*

"That's right." He nodded, wondering if Sonny recognized that as an affirmative sign. "Like big wheelbarrow."

One thing puzzled Sonny, though. Wheelbarrow wheels were small — his hands indicated the size — and single. These were big, and double.

"Let me show you this, Sonny."

He squatted, took a pad and pencil from his pocket, and drew two pairs of wheels, and then put a wagon on them, and drew a quadruped hitched to it, and a Svant with a stick walking beside it. Sonny looked at the picture — Svants seemed to have pictoral sense, for which make us thankful! — and then caught his mother's sleeve and showed it to her. Mom didn't get it. Sonny took the pencil and drew another animal, with a pole travois. He made gestures. A travois dragged; it went slow. A wagon had wheels that went around; it went fast.

So Lillian and Anna thought he was the village half-wit. Village genius, more likely; the other peasants didn't understand him, and resented his superiority. They went over for a closer look at the wheels, and pushed them. Sonny was almost beside himself. Mom was puzzled, but she thought they were pretty wonderful.

Then they looked at blacksmith tools. Tongs; Sonny had never seen anything like them. Howell wondered what the Svants used to handle hot metal; probably big tweezers made by tying two green sticks together. There was an old Arabian legend that Allah had made the first tongs and given them to the first smith, because nobody could make tongs without having a pair already.

Sonny didn't understand the fan-blower until it was taken apart. Then he made a great discovery. The wheels, and the fan, and the pivoted tongs, all embodied the same principle, one his people had evidently never discovered. A whole new world seemed to open before him; from then on, he was constantly finding things pierced and rotating on pivots.

*B*y this time, Mom was fidgeting again. She ought to be doing something to justify her presence in the camp. He was wondering what sort of work he could invent for her when Karl Dorver called to him from the door of the headquarters hut.

"Mark, can you spare Mom for a while?" he asked. "We want her to look at pictures and show us which of the animals are meat-cattle, and which of the crops are ripe."

"Think you can get anything out of her?"

"Sign-talk, yes. We may get a few words from her, too."

At first, Mom was unwilling to leave Sonny. She finally decided that it would be safe, and trotted over to Dorver, entering the hut.

Dave Questell's construction crew began at once on the water tank, using a power shovel to dig the foundation. They had to haul water in a tank from the river a quarter-mile away to mix the concrete. Sonny watched that interestedly. So did a number of the villagers, who gathered safely out of bowshot. They noticed Sonny among the Terrans and pointed at him. Sonny noticed that. He unobtrusively picked up a double-bitted ax and kept it to hand.

He and Mom had lunch with the contact team. As they showed no ill effects from breakfast, Fayon decided that it was safe to let them have anything the Terrans ate or drank. They liked wine; they knew what it was, all right, but this seemed to have a delightfully different flavor. They each tried a cigarette, choked over the first few puffs, and decided that they didn't like smoking.

"Mom gave us a lot of information, as far as she could, on the crops and animals. The big things, the size of rhinoceroses, are draft animals and nothing else; they're not eaten," Dorver said. "I don't know whether the meat isn't good, or is taboo, or they are too valuable to eat. They eat all the other three species, and milk two of them. I have an idea they grind their grain in big stone mortars as needed."

That was right; he'd seen things like that.

"Willi, when you're over in the mountains, see if you can find something we can make millstones out of. We can shape them with sono-cutters; after they get the idea, they can do it themselves by hand. One of those big animals could be used to turn the mill. Did you get any words from her?"

Paul Meillard shook his head gloomily. "Nothing we can be sure of. It was the same thing as in the village, yesterday. She'd say something, I'd repeat it, and she'd tell us it was wrong and say the same thing over again. Lillian took recordings; she got the same results as last night. Ask her about it later."

"She has the same effect on Mom as on the others?"

"Yes. Mom was very polite and tried not to show it, but —"

Lillian took him aside, out of earshot of the two Svants, after lunch. She was almost distracted.

"Mark, I don't know what I'm going to do. She's like the others. Every time I open my mouth in front of her, she's simply horrified. It's as though my voice does something loathsome to her. And I'm the one who's supposed to learn to talk to them."

"Well, those who can do, and those who can't teach," he told her. "You can study recordings, and tell us what the words are and teach us how to recognize and pronounce them. You're the only linguist we have."

That seemed to comfort her a little. He hoped it would work out that way. If they could communicate with these people and did leave a party here to prepare for the first colonization, he'd stay on, to teach the natives Terran technologies and study theirs. He'd been expecting that Lillian would stay, too. She was the linguist; she'd have to stay. But now, if it turned out that she would be no help but a liability, she'd go back with the *Hubert Penrose*. Paul wouldn't keep a linguist who offended the natives' every sensibility with every word she spoke. He didn't want that to happen. Lillian and he had come to mean a little too much to each other to be parted now.

*P*aul Meillard and Karl Dorver had considerable difficulty with Mom, that afternoon. They wanted her to go with them and help trade for cattle. Mom didn't want to; she was afraid. They had to do a lot of play-acting, with half a dozen Marines pretending to guard her with fixed bayonets from some of Dave Questell's Navy construction men who had red bandannas on their heads to simulate combs before she got the idea. Then she was afraid to get into the contragravity lorry that was to carry the hoes and the wagon wheels. Sonny managed to reassure her, and insisted on going along, and he insisted on taking his ax with him. That meant doubling the guard, to make sure Sonny didn't lose his self-control when he saw his former persecutors within chopping distance.

It went off much better than either Paul Meillard or Luis Gofredo expected. After the first shock of being air-borne had worn off, Mom found that she liked contragravity-riding; Sonny was wildly delighted with it from the start. The natives showed neither of them any hostility. Mom's lavender bathrobe and Sonny's green coveralls and big ax seemed to be symbols of a new and exalted status; even the Lord Mayor was extremely polite to them.

The Lord Mayor and half a dozen others got a contragravity ride, too, to the meadows to pick out cattle. A dozen animals, including a pair of the two-ton draft beasts, were driven to the Terran camp. A couple of lorry-loads of assorted vegetables were brought in, too. Everybody seemed very happy about the deal, especially Bennet Fayon. He wanted to slaughter one of the sheep-sized meat-and-milk animals at once and get to work on it. Gofredo advised him to put it off till the next morning. He wanted a large native audience to see the animal being shot with a rifle.

The water tower was finished, and the big spherical tank hoisted on top of it and made fast. A pump, and a filter-system were installed. There was no water for hot showers that evening, though. They would have to run a pipeline to the river, and that would entail a ditch that would cut through several cultivated fields, which, in turn, would provoke an uproar. Paul Meillard didn't want that happening until he'd concluded the cattle-trade.

Charley Loughran and Willi Schallenmacher had gone up to the ship on one of the landing craft; they accompanied the landing party that went down into the mountains. Ayesha Keithley arrived late in the afternoon on another landing craft, with five or six tons of instruments and parts and equipment, and a male Navy warrant-officer helper.

They looked around the lab Lillian had been using at one end of the headquarters hut.

"This won't do," the girl Navy officer said. "We can't get a quarter of the apparatus we're going to need in here. We'll have to build something."

Dave Questell was drawn into the discussion. Yes, he could put up something big enough for everything the girls would need to install, and soundproof it. Concrete, he decided; they'd have to wait till he got the water line down and the pump going, though.

There was a crowd of natives in the fields, gaping at the Terran camp, the next morning, and Gofredo decided to kill the animal – until they learned the native name, they were calling it Domesticated Type C. It was herded out where everyone could watch, and a Marine stepped forward unslung his rifle took a kneeling position, and aimed at it. It was a hundred and fifty yards away. Mom had come out to see what was going on; Sonny and Howell, who had been consulting by signs over the construction of a wagon, were standing side by side. The Marine squeezed his trigger. The rifle banged, and the Domesticated-C bounded into the air, dropped, and kicked a few times and was still. The natives, however, missed that part of it; they were howling piteously and rubbing their heads. All but Sonny. He was just mildly surprised at what had happened to the Dom.-C.

Sonny, it would appear, was stone deaf.

*A*s anticipated, there was another uproar later in the morning when the ditching machine started north across the meadow. A mob of Svants, seeing its relentless progress toward a field of something like turnips, gathered in front of it, twittering and brandishing implements of agriculture, many of them Terran-made.

Paul Meillard was ready for this. Two lorries went out; one loaded with Marines, who jumped off with their rifles ready. By this time, all the Svants knew what rifles would do beside make a noise. Meillard, Dorver, Gofredo and a few others got out of the other vehicle, and unloaded presents. Gofredo did all the talking. The Svants couldn't understand him, but they liked it. They also liked the presents, which included a dozen empty half-gallon rum demijohns, tarpaulins, and a lot of assorted knickknacks. The pipeline went through.

He and Sonny got the forge set up. There was no fuel for it. A party of Marines had gone out to the woods to the east to cut wood; when they got back, they'd burn some charcoal in the pit that had been dug beside the camp. Until then, he and Sonny were drawing plans for a wooden wheel with a metal tire when Lillian came out of the headquarters hut with a clipboard under her arm. She motioned to him.

"Come on over," he told her. "You can talk in front of Sonny; he won't mind. He can't hear."

"Can't hear?" she echoed. "You mean — ?"

"That's right. Sonny's stone deaf. He didn't even hear that rifle going off. The only one of this gang that has brains enough to pour sand out of a boot with directions on the bottom of the heel, and he's a total linguistic loss."

"So he isn't a half-wit, after all."

"He's got an IQ close to genius level. Look at this; he never saw a wheel before yesterday; now he's designing one."

Lillian's eyes widened. "So that's why Mom's so sharp about sign-talk. She's been doing it all his life." Then she remembered what she had come out to show him, and held out the clipboard. "You know how that analyzer of mine works? Well, here's what Ayesha's going to do. After breaking a sound into frequency bands instead of being photographed and projected, each band goes to an analyzer of its own, and is projected on its own screen. There'll be forty of them, each for a band of a hundred cycles, from zero to four thousand. That seems to be the Svant vocal range."

The diagram passed from hand to hand during cocktail time, before dinner. Bennet Fayon had been working all day dissecting the animal they were all calling a *domsee*, a name which would stick even if and when they learned the native name. He glanced disinterestedly at the drawing, then looked again, more closely. Then he set down the drink he was holding in his other hand and studied it intently.

"You know what you have here?" he asked. "This is a very close analogy to the hearing organs of that animal I was working on. The comb, as we've assumed, is the external organ. It's covered with small flaps and fissures. Back of each fissure is a long, narrow membrane; they're paired, one on each side of the comb, and from them nerves lead to clusters of small round membranes. Nerves lead from them to a complex nerve-cable at the bottom of the comb and into the brain at the base of the skull. I couldn't understand how the system functioned, but now I see it. Each of the larger membranes on the outside responds to a sound-frequency band, and the small ones on the inside break the bands down to individual frequencies."

"How many of the little ones are there?" Ayesha asked.

"Thousands of them; the inner comb is simply packed with them. Wait; I'll show you."

He rose and went away, returning with a sheaf of photo-enlargements and a number of blocks of Lucite in which specimens were mounted. Everybody examined them. Anna de Jong, as a practicing psychologist, had an M.D. and to get that she'd had to know a modicum of anatomy; she was puzzled.

"I can't understand how they hear with those things. I'll grant that the membranes will respond to sound, but I can't see how they transmit it."

"But they do hear," Meillard said. "Their musical instruments, their reactions to our voices, the way they are affected by sounds like gunfire —"

"They hear, but they don't hear in the same way we do," Fayon replied. "If you can't be convinced by anything else, look at these things, and compare them with the structure of the human ear, or the ear of any member of any other sapient race we're ever contacted. That's what I've been saying from the beginning."

"They have sound-perception to an extent that makes ours look almost like deafness," Ayesha Keithley said. "I wish I could design a sound-detector one-tenth as good as this must be."

Yes. The way the Lord Mayor said *fwoonk* and the way Paul Meillard said it sounded entirely different to them. Of course, *fwoonk* and *pwink* and *tweelt* and *kroosh* sounded alike to them, but let's don't be too picky about things.

*T*here were no hot showers that evening; Dave Questell's gang had trouble with the pump and needed some new parts made up aboard the ship. They were still working on it the next morning. He had meant to start teaching Sonny blacksmithing, but during the evening Lillian and Anna had decided to try teaching Mom a nonphonetic, ideographic, alphabet, and in the morning they co-opted Sonny to help. Deprived of his disciple, he strolled over to watch the work on the pump. About twenty Svants had come in from the fields and were also watching, from the meadow.

After a while, the job was finished. The petty officer in charge of the work pushed in the switch, and the pump started, sucking dry with a harsh racket. The natives twittered in surprise. Then the water came, and the pump settled down to a steady *thugg-thugg, thugg-thugg.*

The Svants seemed to like the new sound; they grimaced in pleasure and moved closer; within forty or fifty feet, they all squatted on the ground and sat entranced. Others came in from the fields, drawn by the sound. They, too, came up and squatted, until there was a semicircle of them. The tank took a long time to fill; until it did, they all sat immobile and fascinated. Even after it stopped, many remained, hoping that it would start again. Paul Meillard began wondering, a trifle uneasily, if that would happen every time the pump went on.

"They get a positive pleasure from it. It affects them the same way Luis' voice does."

"Mean I have a voice like a pump?" Gofredo demanded.

"Well, I'm going to find out," Ayesha Keithley said. "The next time that starts, I'm going to make a recording, and compare it with your voice-recording. I'll give five to one there'll be a similarity."

Questell got the foundation for the sonics lab dug, and began pouring concrete. That took water, and the pump ran continuously that afternoon. Concrete-mixing took more water the next day, and by noon the whole village population, down to the smallest child, was massed at the pumphouse, enthralled. Mom was snared by the sound like any of the rest; only Sonny was unaffected. Lillian and Ayesha compared recordings of the voices of the team with the pump-sound; in Gofredo's they found an identical frequency-pattern.

"We'll need the new apparatus to be positive about it, but it's there, all right," Ayesha said. "That's why Luis' voice pleases them."

"That tags me; Old Pump-Mouth," Gofredo said. "It'll get all through the Corps, and they'll be calling me that when I'm a four-star general, if I live that long."

Meillard was really worried, now. So was Bennet Fayon. He said so that afternoon at cocktail time.

"It's an addiction," he declared. "Once they hear it, they have no will to resist; they just squat and listen. I don't know what it's doing to them, but I'm scared of it."

"I know one thing it's doing," Meillard said. "It's keeping them from their work in the fields. For all we know, it may cause them to lose a crop they need badly for subsistence."

The native they had come to call the Lord Mayor evidently thought so, too. He was with the others, the next morning, squatting with his staff across his knees, as bemused as any of them, but when the pump stopped he rose and approached a group of Terrans, launching into what could only be an impassioned tirade. He pointed with his staff to the pump house, and to the semicircle of still motionless villagers. He pointed to the fields, and back to the people, and to the pump house again, gesturing vehemently with his other hand.

You make the noise. My people will not work while they hear it. The fields lie untended. Stop the noise, and let my people work.

Couldn't possibly be any plainer.

Then the pump started again. The Lord Mayor's hands tightened on the staff; he was struggling tormentedly with himself, in vain. His face relaxed into the heartbroken expression of joy; he turned and shuffled over, dropping onto his haunches with the others.

"Shut down the pump, Dave!" Meillard called out. "Cut the power off."

The *thugg-thugg*-ing stopped. The Lord Mayor rose, made an odd salaamlike bow toward the Terrans, and then turned on the people, striking with his staff and shrieking at them. A few got to their feet and joined him, screaming, pushing, tugging. Others joined. In a little while, they were all on their feet, straggling away across the fields.

Dave Questell wanted to know what it meant; Meillard explained.

"Well, what are we going to do for water?" the Navy engineer asked.

"Soundproof the pump house. You can do that, can't you?"

"Sure. Mound it over with earth. We'll have that done in a few hours."

That started Gofredo worrying. "This happens every time we colonize an inhabited planet. We give the natives something new. Then we find out it's bad for them, and we try to take it away from them. And then the knives come out, and the shooting starts."

Luis Gofredo was also a specialist, speaking on his subject.

*W*hile they were at lunch, Charley Loughran screened in from the other camp and wanted to talk to Bennet Fayon.

"A funny thing, Bennet. I took a shot at a bird . . . no, a flying mammal . . . and dropped it. It was dead when it hit the ground, but there isn't a mark on it. I want you to do an autopsy, and find out how I can kill things by missing them."

"How far away was it?"

"Call it forty feet; no more."

"What were you using, Charley?" Ayesha Keithley called from the table.

"Eight-point-five Mars-Consolidated pistol," Loughran said. "I'd laid my shotgun down and walked away from it —"

"Twelve hundred foot-seconds," Ayesha said. "Bow-wave as well as muzzle-blast."

"You think the report was what did it?" Fayon asked.

"You want to bet it didn't?" she countered.

Nobody did.

*M*om was sulky. She didn't like what Dave Questell's men were doing to the nice-noise-place. Ayesha and Lillian consoled her by taking her into the soundproofed room and playing the recording of the pump-noise for her. Sonny couldn't care less, one way or another; he spent the afternoon teaching Mark Howell what the marks on paper meant. It took a lot of signs and play-acting. He had learned about thirty ideographs; by combining them and drawing little pictures, he could express a number of simple ideas. There was, of course, a limit to how many of those things anybody could learn and remember — look how long it took an Old Terran

Chinese scribe to learn his profession — but it was the beginning
of a method of communication.

Questell got the pump house mounded over. Ayesha came out
and tried a sound-meter, and also Mom, on it while the pump was
running. Neither reacted.

A good many Svants were watching the work. They began to
demonstrate angrily. A couple tried to interfere and were knocked
down with rifle butts. The Lord Mayor and his Board of Aldermen
came out with the big horn and harangued them at length, and
finally got them to go back to the fields. As nearly as anybody
could tell, he was friendly to and co-operative with the Terrans.
The snooper over the village reported excitement in the plaza.

Bennet Fayon had taken an airjeep to the other camp immediately after lunch. He was back by 1500, accompanied by Loughran.
They carried a cloth-wrapped package into Fayon's dissecting-
room. At cocktail time, Paul Meillard had to go and get them.

"Sorry," Fayon said, joining the group. "Didn't notice how late
it was getting. We're still doing a post on this svant-bat; that's what
Charley's calling it, till we get the native name."

"The immediate cause of death was spasmodic contraction of
every muscle in the thing's body; some of them were partly relaxed
before we could get to work on it, but not completely. Every bone
that isn't broken is dislocated; a good many both. There is not the
slightest trace of external injury. Everything was done by its own
muscles." He looked around. "I hope nobody covered Ayesha's
bet, after I left. If they did, she collects. The large outer membranes
in the comb seem to be unaffected, but there is considerable
compression of the small round ones inside, in just one area, and
more on the left side than on the right. Charley says it was flying
across in front of him from left to right."

"The receptor-area responding to the frequencies of the report,"
Ayesha said.

Anna de Jong made a passing gesture toward Fayon. "The baby's
yours, Bennet," she said. "This isn't psychological. I won't accept
a case of psychosomatic compound fracture."

"Don't be too premature about it, Anna. I think that's more or
less what you have, here."

Everybody looked at him, surprised. His subject was compara-
tive technology. The bio- and psychosciences were completely
outside his field.

"A lot of things have been bothering me, ever since the first
contact. I'm beginning to think I'm on the edge of understanding
them, now. Bennet, the higher life-forms here — the people, and

that domsee, and Charley's svant-bat — are structurally identical with us. I don't mean gross structure, like ears and combs. I mean molecular and cellular and tissue structure. Is that right?"

Fayon nodded. "Biology on this planet is exactly Terra type. Yes. With adequate safeguards, I'd even say you could make a viable tissue-graft from a Svant to a Terran, or vice versa."

"Ayesha, would the sound waves from that pistol-shot in any conceivable way have the sort of physical effect we're considering?"

"Absolutely not," she said, and Luis Gofredo said: "I've been shot at and missed with pistols at closer range than that."

"Then it was the effect on the animal's nervous system."

Anna shrugged. "It's still Bennet's baby. I'm a psychologist, not a neurologist."

"What I've been saying, all along," Fayon reiterated complacently. "Their hearing is different from ours. This proves it.

"It proves that they don't hear at all."

He had expected an explosion; he wasn't disappointed. They all contradicted him, many derisively. Signal reactions. Only Paul Meillard made the semantically appropriate response:

"What do you mean, Mark?"

"They don't *hear* sound; they *feel* it. You all saw what they have inside their combs. Those things don't transmit sound like the ears of any sound-sensitive life-form we've ever seen. They transform sound waves into tactile sensations."

Fayon cursed, slowly and luridly. Anna de Jong looked at him wide-eyed. He finished his cocktail and poured another. In the snooper screen, what looked like an indignation meeting was making uproar in the village plaza. Gofredo cut the volume of the speaker even lower.

"That would explain a lot of things," Meillard said slowly. "How hard it was for them to realize that we didn't understand when they talked to us. A punch in the nose feels the same to anybody. They thought they were giving us bodily feelings. They didn't know we were insensible to them."

"But they do . . . they do have a language," Lillian faltered. "They talk."

"Not the way we understand it. If they want to say, 'Me,' it's *tickle-pinch-rub*, even if it sounds like *fwoonk* to us, when it doesn't sound like *pwink* or *tweelt* or *kroosh*. The tactile sensations, to a Svant, feel no more different than a massage by four different hands. Analogous to a word pronounced by four different voices, to us. They'll have a code for expressing meanings in tactile sensation, just as we have a code for expressing meanings in audible sound."

"Except that when a Svant tells another, 'I am happy,' or 'I have a stomach-ache,' he makes the other one feel that way too," Anna said. "That would carry an awful lot more conviction. I don't imagine symptom-swapping is popular among Svants. Karl! You were nearly right, at that. This isn't telepathy, but it's a lot like it."

"So it is," Dorver, who had been mourning his departed telepathy theory, said brightly. "And look how it explains their society. Peaceful, everybody in quick agreement —" He looked at the screen and gulped. The Lord Mayor and his party had formed one clump, and the opposition was grouped at the other side of the plaza; they were screaming in unison at each other. "They make their decisions by endurance; the party that can resist the feelings of the other longest converts their opponents."

"Pure democracy," Gofredo declared. "Rule by the party that can make the most noise."

"And I'll bet that when they're sick, they go around chanting, 'I am well; I feel just fine!'" Anna said. "Autosuggestion would really work, here. Think of the feedback, too. One Svant has a feeling. He verbalizes it, and the sound of his own voice re-enforces it in him. It is induced in his hearers, and they verbalize it, re-enforcing it in themselves and in him. This could go on and on."

"Yes. It has. Look at their technology." He felt more comfortable, now he was on home ground again. "A friend of mine, speaking about a mutual acquaintance, once said, 'When they installed her circuits, they put in such big feeling circuits that there was no room left for any thinking circuits.' I think that's a perfect description of what I estimate Svant mentality to be. Take these bronze knives, and the musical instruments. Wonderful; the work of individuals trying to express feeling in metal or wood. But get an idea like the wheel, or even a pair of tongs? Poo! How would you state the First Law of Motion, or the Second Law of Thermodynamics, in tickle-pinch-rub terms? Sonny could grasp an idea like that. Sonny's handicap, if you call it that, cuts him off from feel-thinking; he can think logically instead of sensually."

He sipped his cocktail and continued: "I can understand why the village is mounded up, too. I realized that while I was watching Dave's gang bury the pump house. I'd been bothered by that, and by the absence of granaries for all the grain they raise, and by the number of people for so few and such small houses. I think the village is mostly underground, and the houses are just entrances, soundproofed, to shelter them from uncomfortable natural noises? — ?thunderstorms, for instance."

The horn was braying in the snooper-screen speaker; somebody wondered what it was for. Gofredo laughed.

"I thought, at first, that it was a war-horn. It isn't. It's a peace-horn," he said. "Public tranquilizer. The first day, they brought it out and blew it at us to make us peaceable."

"Now I see why Sonny is rejected and persecuted," Anna was saying. "He must make all sorts of horrible noises that he can't hear . . . that's not the word; we have none for it . . . and nobody but his mother can stand being near him."

"Like me," Lillian said. "Now I understand. Just think of the most revolting thing that could be done to you physically; that's what I do to them every time I speak. And I always thought I had a nice voice," she added, pathetically.

"You have, for Terrans," Ayesha said. "For Svants, you'll just have to change it."

"But how — ?"

"Use an analyzer; train it. That was why I took up sonics, in the first place. I had a voice like a crow with a sore throat, but by practicing with an analyzer, an hour a day, I gave myself an entirely different voice in a couple of months. Just try to get some pump-sound frequencies into it, like Luis'."

"But why? I'm no use here. I'm a linguist, and these people haven't any language that I could ever learn, and they couldn't even learn ours. They couldn't learn to make sounds, as sounds."

"You've been doing very good work with Mom on those ideo-graphs," Meillard said. "Keep it up till you've taught her the Lingua Terra Basic vocabulary, and with her help we can train a few more. They can be our interpreters; we can write what we want them to say to the others. It'll be clumsy, but it will work, and it's about the only thing I can think of that will."

"And it will improve in time," Ayesha added. "And we can make vocoders and visibilizers. Paul, you have authority to requisition personnel from the ship's company. Draft me; I'll stay here and work on it."

The rumpus in the village plaza was getting worse. The Lord Mayor and his adherents were being out-shouted by the opposition.

"Better do something about that in a hurry, Paul, if you don't want a lot of Svants shot," Gofredo said. "Give that another half hour and we'll have visitors, with bows and spears."

"Ayesha, you have a recording of the pump," Meillard said. "Load a record-player onto a jeep and fly over the village and play it for them. Do it right away. Anna, get Mom in here. We want to get her to tell that gang that from now on, at noon and for a couple of hours after sunset, when the work's done, there will be free public pump-concerts, over the village plaza."

*A*yesha and her warrant-officer helper and a Marine lieutenant went out hastily. Everybody else faced the screen to watch. In fifteen minutes, an airjeep was coming in on the village. As it circled low, a new sound, the steady *thugg-thugg, thugg-thugg* of the pump, began.

The yelling and twittering and the blaring of the peace-horn died out almost at once. As the jeep circled down to housetop level, the two contending faction-clumps broke apart; their component individuals moved into the center of the plaza and squatted, staring up, letting the delicious waves of sound caress them.

"Do we have to send a detail in a jeep to do that twice a day?" Gofredo asked. "We keep a snooper over the village; fit it with a loud-speaker and a timer; it can give them their *thugg-thugg,* on schedule, automatically."

"We might give the Lord Mayor a recording and a player and let him decide when the people ought to listen — if that's the word — to it," Dorver said. "Then it would be something of their own."

"No!" He spoke so vehemently that the others started. "You know what would happen? Nobody would be able to turn it off; they'd all be hypnotized, or doped, or whatever it is. They'd just sit in a circle around it till they starved to death, and when the power-unit gave out, the record-player would be surrounded by a ring of skeletons. We'll just have to keep on playing it for them ourselves. Terrans' Burden."

"That'll give us a sanction over them," Gofredo observed. "Extra *thugg-thugg* if they're very good; shut it off on them if they act nasty. And find out what Lillian has in her voice that the rest of us don't have, and make a good loud recording of that, and stash it away along with the rest of the heavy-weapons ammunition. You know, you're not going to have any trouble at all, when we go down-country to talk to the king or whatever. This is better than fire-water ever was."

"We must never misuse our advantage, Luis," Meillard said seriously. "We must use it only for their good."

He really meant it. Only — You had to know some general history to study technological history, and it seemed to him that that pious assertion had been made a few times before. Some of the others who had made it had really meant it, too, but that had made little difference in the long run.

Fayon and Anna were talking enthusiastically about the work ahead of them.

"I don't know where your subject ends and mine begins," Anna was saying. "We'll just have to handle it between us. What are we going to call it? We certainly can't call it hearing."

"Nonauditory sonic sense is the only thing I can think of," Fayon said. "And that's such a clumsy term."

"Mark; you thought of it first," Anna said. "What do you think?"

"Nonauditory sonic sense. It isn't any worse than Domesticated Type C, and that got cut down to size. *Naudsonce.*"

Printed in the United States
88216LV00004B/111/A

9 781598 183610